Model Citizens

BY ~~Paul Anderson~~

Lauren,

Thank you for putting that cot in the back of your van so I have a place to sleep when Megan kicks me out. Enjoy the book!

Paul And—

Copyright © 2015 by Paul Anderson

All rights reserved. No part of this publication may be reproduced, distributed, or transmitted in any form or by any means, including photocopying, recording, or other electronic or mechanical methods, without the prior written permission of the publisher, except in the case of brief quotations embodied in critical reviews and certain other noncommercial uses permitted by copyright law. For permission requests, write to the publisher, addressed "Attention: Permissions Coordinator," at the address below.

Wordpool Press
10970 196th Ave.
Big Rapids, MI 49307

www.wordpoolpress.com

Published by: Wordpool Press
Original Cover Art by: Paul Anderson
Anderson, Paul, Model Citizens

ISBN-10: 0-9905888-3-1
ISBN-13: 978-0-9905888-3-2

10 9 8 7 6 5 4 3 2
1. fiction 2. short story collection

First Edition

Ordering Information:
Quantity sales. Special discounts are available on quantity purchases by corporations, associations, and others. For details, contact the publisher at the address above.

Printed in the United States of America

ACKNOWLEDGMENTS

"The Name" and "I Must Be God" were originally published in *Temenos*; "As for Me…" was originally published in *Gravel*.

I'd like to extend a heartfelt thank you to my family, friends, and mentors. I could not have completed this collection without your patience and support. Your kind words and advice truly mean the world to me. I'd also like to extend a special thank you to my BA, MA, and MFA mentors: Judy Kerman and Vince Samarco of Saginaw Valley State University; Darrin Doyle, Melinda Kreth, and Matt Roberson of Central Michigan University; and Diane Payne and Adam Prince of University of Arkansas-Monticello. To my mom, Sally, my dad, Dave, and my siblings, Steffanie and Joey: thank you for your unending love, support, and inspiration. To my wife, Megan: thank you for giving me the strength and confidence to complete this collection, and for keeping me motivated, even when it meant you'd have to do more housework. You truly are the best thing that's ever happened to me.

TABLE OF CONTENTS

I Must Be God	1
Twenty-one Seconds a Night-Light	14
The Name	41
As for Me...	48
Campfire in Africa	89
Spiral	101
Advent	141

For Megan

I Must Be God

A line of trees rushes past. I can almost hear the wind pressing through them. The leaves are changing colors. Some of them are falling off. I think about one of them, a special leaf from my imagination. This leaf dangles and flaps before a gust plucks it away. It becomes a spinning ballerina. The long grass on the hillside folds over. This is the wind revealing its shape. "See?" I say. "Even the wind needs rest."

I've often wondered why, of all the infinity of colors, green is the earth's first choice. Leaves, grass, even the sea — all some shade of green. And what of primary colors? Why not blue, or yellow?

"Just drive," Panda says. He's picking his tooth with Dad's old jackknife. It has a mahogany handle and a gold blade. The gold is fake, but it looks appealing. This was Dad's only gift to us. It was a parting gift. Dad used it to carve wood. Once, he used it to cut out a bunch of kittens from their mama's belly. "What goes around comes around," he said. I always took that to mean history repeats itself.

I never knew why Dad cut that cat open. Killing helpless creatures is so unnatural. There were four babies. Panda and I raised them until they died a couple years later, when I was nine. I am twenty-seven now. I could have raised lots of kittens.

Panda says, "Do your job. Both hands on the wheel."

I steer with one hand. I let the other one rest. This is my way. My right hand is a spider on the center console. I watch Panda suck down the rest of his vodka in the rearview. I'm thirsty.

"You're lucky we brought you," I tell him, but he is my older brother. Mom drank while she was pregnant with him, so his thinking is wrong. I bring him with me when I can. I do this to fix him. I am his surgeon.

"I envy you, Toby," Haley says to me. "You've never been sad before."

Haley rides the El sometimes. I remember how she was doubled over in her seat. She had slender arms folded across her belly. There was a tattoo on her right forearm. It was a monarch butterfly, as orange and black as Halloween. It seemed to have been pinned there. I saw a couple track marks near it, black pinholes atop raised skin. They looked like anthills. I kept waiting for a colony to crawl out. I couldn't stop staring — it was all so natural.

Panda prefers the backseat. "I don't believe in ghosts," he says. It's a voice over my shoulder, like a memory. We're a couple hours northwest of Chicago on I-90, heading towards Wisconsin. Panda waves a stubby finger in the rearview and tells me, "Keep driving. Gotta get north."

"Trees are like guardians," I say.

"Forward, forward," he says. "Yeah."

Haley prefers the seat next to me. She's zoned out with her cheek on the glass. She shoots up a couple times a day. I like the way her hair goes black when she's high. I just love that kind of moisture.

"It might snow soon," she whispers.

"It's a misconception," I tell her. "Don't let those clouds trick you."

She closes her eyes. "I can't see them anymore. Okay?" Purple fingernails zigzag over her face. She's only a mouth now. She has the whitest teeth. She bit my neck last night in bed, and I thought the color would seep out of my skin.

"I feel like sand," Panda says. He presses his palm against his forehead. "There's grains coming out of me." He's getting frantic. He pounds his fist repeatedly against his thigh. This is common, so I ignore it. Haley is oblivious.

I press my foot down for speed. I should have worn shoes today. Tiny rocks press into my calluses. It's a numb feeling. "The lake will be cold," I remind them. "Water gets really cold this time of year."

Haley was all strung out on the El. It rattled and clanked around on the track. Her body bounced back and forth. She had lost all control. But there were these two teenage boys making out in the back. Their faces were soft. One of them had precise hands. He was in control of the moment. I think I wanted to kill him.

"Maybe they're angels," Haley says. She's smiling now.

"Who's that?" Panda asks.

"The trees," she answers.

"Ain't no such thing as angels," Panda retorts.

Haley turns in her seat and glares at him. "They both stay with you until their feathers fall off."

My mom smoked cigarettes when she was pregnant with me. One of my ears is bigger than the other one. I have trouble pronouncing the letter "r" sometimes. I think it's because she smoked. But I'm okay with it. It's an innocent addiction. She had rights.

Haley's belly is a cantaloupe. In a couple of months it will be a watermelon. Panda likes peach schnapps. People are obsessed with fruits. We name our drinks, our lip balm, our perfumes, even our children after them. I like nature. I'm really no different.

I was with Haley at a restaurant downtown. We were somewhere near Lake Michigan. The water was so blue you could hardly tell where it ended and the sky began. It was all so analogous. Panda had stayed at the apartment. Haley was spaced out. She had trouble chewing her pizza. She kept talking about the beauty of deep dish — not the food, but the words. "They fit together," she told me. Her eyes were black. I think her pupils were dilated.

"Like holding hands," I agreed.

"The El was our special place," she explained. She was talking about Len, her ex. "We would go there, and it would take us to this road in heaven, just up into the clouds. Don't they look like giant brains?"

Len was gone by then. He was just a word to me. He had no face. He may as well have been dead.

"This is what babies do," I explained. "This is how you scare us away."

"Cloud brains," she whispered, and giggled. She couldn't hear me — her ears were tuned to a different station. Then she reached for my hand. She was already getting motherly. "I don't miss him. His skin felt like bread crust."

I stared at her track marks. She had reused the same holes. She'd probably done so twenty times by now. I thought I could feel the drug seeping out of her skin. I rubbed her palm.

"Where can I get some?"

I could tell she wanted to be a drooling mess. She scrunched up her nose and bit her lip, showing snowy teeth, so happy and nostalgic all of a sudden. "I'll show you the way, and you'll never wanna come back," she teased.

"I'll love you forever," I promised, and it was then that I knew I was a father.

The highway unfolds before me, and I'm just sober enough to traverse the distance. At the border we pay the toll and cross into Wisconsin where the hills are white . . . like elephants. There was a story I read a hundred years ago, this story about hills and people talking in a diner. I think that could be Haley and me. I think that's when things began to lose color, back when I read that. The hills here are green and sometimes yellow, but white means lifeless, and elephants are enormous. I think I'd like a change in weather. Funny how tiny snowflakes are but how big a blanket they can weave.

Passing vehicles hide mysteries. I can't see faces; I only see a flash of colors whizzing towards me. There are no connections to be made. This old station wagon is our world. There is very little nature here. Even the air is

7

false. I don't know how we're breathing.

"Mushrooms," I say. "Stuff like that. I prefer earthly drugs."

"They're all from earth," Haley jokes.

Panda is a whale on the backseat, floundering. His breathing is wet. He is too drunk for consciousness. He's above life right now. He is angelic.

"I've always been naive about this," I tell her.

Haley directs me down a wooded path. For a few hundred yards, there are rainbows of leaves dancing around us. Then a clearing opens up, and we come to a tiny unpainted shack. It's just a big box composed of gray boards. The yard is all dirt and yellow weeds.

"This is it?" I ask. "This is the lake?" There appears to be a very small pond out back a ways. It's more of a gigantic puddle with a throng of cattails protruding from it like whiskers. There's something very dead about the place, here in the foreground, against a backdrop of bright trees.

Haley giggles and bites her knuckle. Suddenly her butterfly tattoo is staring at me. I wonder if all the world's pictures have eyes like this. My two weeks with Haley may as well be two hundred years. We are a thing now. I am the father of her child, and I am worthy of the task because it isn't composed of my blood. This is our life now, this dead place drawn up in earth tones, and I am momentarily overwhelmed.

"We'll grow gardens here," I tell her. "Crops and drugs." I point to the pond. "We'll build a dock for our kid to play on."

Haley gazes out the windshield. She seems sober. Her eyes are green and all-encompassing. "Len took me to a meeting once. It was right when I got pregnant."

"A meeting? For your addiction?"

But she doesn't answer. She's just a bony heap now. She's locked up. I can't converse with tears.

We share needles for the next three days. We are tenants of the moment. My life has grown into a perpetual instant. It is one event. This is new. I never thought days could drip into one another like syrup. It's as if I can see the future. I must be God.

Panda sleeps in the shack. It has only one room. There is nothing here but drugs, alcohol,

9

and vegetables. We are cannibals because we're a part of nature. Panda, like us, has enjoyed his flavors. These things are our fruits.

Haley and I are fucking by the pond, letting the October air sneak into our flesh. A three-quarter moon is our spotlight. Haley is six months pregnant. I am high on smack and life, and I believe they are one and the same. I keep thinking about the baby pressed between us, rolling around inside Haley's uterus. It's like shaking a giant snow globe. It is beautiful. I want to sink into this place forever.

I begin to exert into her when a faint rustling interrupts me. I look up. Something thumps and shatters against my ear. White glitter spots the night. I hear an odd thwap sound, and then I slip into a dream I can't remember.

I wake up to electricity in my head. The sun is hiding behind a cloud, but the sky is blue. The day is peaceful, but I am sick, down from my high. I might be concussed. My eyes need to adjust.

Something sticky adheres to my head. I touch my temple. I scrape away a blackish film with my thumbnail: dried blood. There's a pile of glass beside me and the faint smell of

10

alcohol.

"I got all grainy again," Panda says. I lift my head just enough to see him sitting there in the sand. He's naked. His fat, hairy chest is covered in something that resembles raspberry filling. He's holding something, cradling it carefully in his arms. He is a gentle soul.

I look to the left. Haley is there, face-down, half in the pond. The sand is black around her. I see Dad's jackknife lying there, glinting more golden than the sun.

"I took out the little babies," Panda explains. "Two little babies all packed up in that skinny cocoon." Panda rocks back and forth. "Do you think they're sleeping? They seem real tired."

I sit up. All the colors of the world drain away. There is an odd pull at my chest, as if someone is tugging on my ventricles. I feel my blood pulse away from my heart. It is raining inside me. My eyes feel hot, and the muscles in my forehead and cheeks grow sore. I begin to wonder if this is what anguish feels like.

Panda sees me. His face contorts. "Did I do wrong?" he asks. I keep staring at Haley. Her upper body bobs up and down in the water. It's as if the pond is licking her.

11

A subtle breeze blows by. My overgrown bangs tickle my face. A yellow leaf dances through the air and lands on Panda's shoulder. It waggles there for a moment before the breeze plucks it away, like a feather. The wind is done resting and Panda is no longer with me. "No," I say to him, getting to my feet. "You made them angels."

"No such thing," he says and laughs. His eyes are wide and happy.

I stamp through the bloody mud. My footprints fill with fluid. It occurs to me that everything is particles, and particles are temporary, but nothing is really temporary after all because nothing really goes away, so temporary is the same as forever. Maybe we live in a giant snow globe, and if the glass breaks it just gets replaced with new glass. Glass is just sand. Panda has sand in him, too, and sand is dust. Maybe everything comes from the dust and if everything comes from the dust then it must return — history must repeat itself. That's the way of nature, I think. It's a big machine that makes being and not being the same thing.

Panda whispers comforts to the silent fetuses: "Shhh," he says, ever so softly. "Shhhhhh..."

I lift the jackknife.

Twenty-one Seconds a Night-light

)—————————————————(

Burnham chomps fry after fry, each freshly removed from the metal basket that now hangs above the bubbling vat of grease. He fights the agonizing heat against his teeth and the soft tissue of his mouth and throat. Each fry is like swallowing a lit match.

The tips of his index finger and thumb are bright red.

"Not again." It's a voice from behind him.

"Hi, Frank," Burnham says without turning around.

"Come on, dude. This has to stop."

Burnham listens to a fry crunch between his molars. His fingers and tongue throb. He stares at the yellowish tendrils of grease that stretch away from the fry basket before detaching and falling into the bubbling pool below.

"You hear me?" Frank says.

"Yes, Frank. I hear you. Jesus."

Frank is a full-timer here at Benny's Burgers, so though he's no older than nineteen or twenty, he thinks he's a boss.

Burnham finally turns and looks at him. He feels tired and annoyed, but thrilled by the prospect of confrontation. An image of Harmony threatens to overwhelm him, but he fights it, suppresses it, focuses his energy on Frank.

Although Frank is clearly Hispanic, Burnham didn't much care about him until a few weeks ago. Burnham had been working the front counter, covering for a coworker, when in walked Frank and his little sister, Anna, who was no older than five. Frank had her up on his shoulders and she was giggling uncontrollably. Frank had introduced her to everyone, including Burnham, who did his best to hide his distaste. Something about the sight of Frank and Anna together — their smiles and the way they

15

clearly cared about each other — had led to a sort of snapping inside Burnham, a weird and frustrating feeling of loss and jealousy.

"I'll tell the boss-lady," Frank says now. "This isn't sanitary."

When Burnham doesn't answer — instead, just stares at him — Frank points at the French fries and continues: "Seriously, dude, if Angie knew you were touching the food it would be your ass."

"Frank," Burnham says, "you're Mexican, right?"

Frank scowls and leans back in an exaggerated way, as if Burnham has just raised a hand to him. "What? Why does it matter?"

Burnham eats a fry. "I'm just curious."

Frank's mouth drops open — the same stupid look he always gets when he's confused: A horse-toothed pink hole in the middle of his bushy face.

Burnham points at the black locks protruding from Frank's red hat and says, "You've got Mexican hair. And you're dark-complected. You look Mexican."

"Well, my mom is Mexican," Frank tells

him. "My grandparents came here in the seventies or something."

Burnham looks down at the grease. He thinks about jabbing his finger in, like he did yesterday. He remembers the sudden pain, how quickly he had to recoil. Frank had somehow seen the whole thing, had come darting over with wide eyes. Burnham remembers Frank's lecture, remembers forcing a smile and slowly plunging his finger in again. He remembers the shock on Frank's face.

The grease bubbles, bubbles, and then Burnham sees a new image: A melting face, cheeks drooping like hot wax.

"Frank," he says. "Stay the hell away from me."

*

Sunlight seeps through the curtains. The room takes on an orange hue. It is both dark and light at the same time.

"Harmony, dear. Where's Harmony?"

"Mom," Burnham says. "Come on. Remember?"

Burnham helps his mother out of her recliner, ignoring the persistent memories of his sister. An infomercial host's excited voice rages out of the old box-shaped television's speakers: "Get our new state-of-the-art wok! Just nineteen-ninety-five! Call *now* and receive a second wok at no cost!"

"Why do you watch this shit?" Burnham says. Images of colorful, steaming vegetables overwhelm the screen.

Lately it's been nothing but infomercials, like this one, and Burnham has begun to wonder if his mother has lost her ability to comprehend stories, if that's why she never watches normal shows anymore.

He leans over and switches the television off before helping her into the wheelchair.

"Do I have cards tonight?"

"Not tonight, Mom."

Burnham begins wheeling her towards the bathroom, ignoring the ancient brown stains — spilled coffee? Pepsi? — in the carpet. He ignores the dead flowers and plants scattered around the house, their browned leaves as crinkly as that cellophane shit they package DVDs and Blu-rays with.

His mother says, "I won at hearts last Saturday. You should've seen it. I shot the moon and Jackie Glennon started running her damn filthy mouth, and then she just stalked off and went home. What a sight it was! Did you know that people…people…um…." Her voice trails off.

"That's nice about your card game, Mom. Wow, good for you."

Fuck me, I need a cigarette, Burnham thinks. His mother's ramblings are commonplace. She tells these tales about people Burnham doesn't even know, her brain misfiring like an old engine, sparking up some random memory of an event that took place decades ago. This time it's card games, probably from the late 1980s or thereabouts, back when Burnham was just a kid. Yesterday it was a fender-bender she had in the parking lot of a grocery store that closed up in 2001. Last week she was going on about Dad winning three-hundred dollars at the casino in Sault Sainte Marie, before Burnham was born. Subsequently, however, Dad had accidentally dropped his wallet into Lake Superior, unwillingly committing his miniscule fortune to the deep.

"Good for me, yes," his mother says. "I usually win, but when I don't, to hell with those bitches!"

The walls of the house make it look like the place fell asleep in 1995 and never woke up. Each room is adorned with flowered wallpaper or borders that long ago began to warp and peel from the walls. The Springy, pastel colors have faded: Some of the yellows appear almost white, or ivory. The flowery designs seem decades outdated. Every time Burnham makes this trek from living room to bathroom, passing through the dining room and kitchen, he is reminded of old commercials from the 90s — commercials he likes to watch on YouTube every now and again. He thinks about how Sprite cans looked so different twenty years ago, or how 90s Ford trucks, so new-looking on the computer screen, still remind him of the weathered rust-buckets he sees in the neighborhood.

"We need to get you in a time machine or something," he tells her as he forces the chair over the threshold, and she begins humming something...a pretty song that he can't place. The lyrics elude him.

"What is that?" he asks, but she doesn't answer, and quickly stops humming.

Once inside the bathroom, Burnham's mother wraps her arms around the back of his neck. He lifts, pulling her to her feet and guiding her until she finds her footing. He helps her lower her drawers and holds her hand to support her until she eases down safely onto the toilet.

"I'll be right out here. I'll leave the door open."

Burnham steps out of the bathroom and into the dining room, which is just a room away, on the other side of the kitchen. He begins poking around the dining table, which is littered with old junk mail, newspapers, and other useless trash.

"We need to throw all this shit away," he says, raising his voice so she'll hear him, but she doesn't answer.

"We could take it all out back and have a nice fire," he says.

He slides a page of expired fast food coupons aside and finds a notepad nestled beneath it. It's one of those notepads with yellow paper. Burnham has always wondered what the use of yellow paper is.

He lifts the notepad and stares at the writing on its top page, a collection of barely-legible cursive squiggles.

She calls from the bathroom: "Bernie? Honey, can you help me now?"

"Just a second, Mom."

He stares at the frantic scrawling on the notepad and notices that it's a series of questions.

"Bernie, are you right there? I can't stand up."

"Yeah, Mom, hang on."

He reads: *Am I sick? Where is Harmony? Is laundry done?*

And down at the bottom: *Will someone please wake me up?*

There is a sudden and familiar *thunk* from the bathroom — the sound of the seat clanking against the porcelain rim of the toilet. Burnham tosses the notepad. He rushes through the kitchen and into the bathroom, expecting to find his mother sprawled out on the floor. Instead, he discovers that she is still in a seated position atop the toilet.

"I fell right back down," she says, her face flushed. She looks pouty, fish-lipped, but there's the faintest evidence of a smile, too.

"Jesus Christ, Mom. Are you okay?"

"I'm fine, but I'm pretty sure my ass'll have

a nice bruise."

Burnham stares at her. Her eyes are locked on his with an intensity and awareness he hasn't seen much for the past couple of years. There's no confused emptiness in them. Instead, they are the oily-colored, expectant eyes of an amateur comedienne waiting for a laugh.

It occurs to him that she is joking around, having a rare moment of clarity. He feels a sense of profound wonder — life is a goddamn funny thing sometimes — but he also feels exposed, on the brink of being found out, though he isn't sure he is hiding anything from her.

"Where have you been?" Burnham says, and for a reason he doesn't quite understand, he punches the wall next to the doorframe.

*

Burnham sits in his gray Malibu across the street from a homey bi-level with beige siding and chocolate-colored shutters. The grass in the yard is dry, yellowed, and the giant maple tree that flanks the house has begun to lose its leaves, though many of them have held onto their greenness with impressive stubbornness. Burnham guesses that less than half of the tree has taken on its usual mid-autumn color, though eventually all of its leaves will be as red as an ocean sunset.

Of course, he can't see any of this detail in the gloom, but he knows from previous visits. Since his mother's moment of clarity a couple weeks ago, he has been stricken by an impatient feeling, as if he needs to act. He's been driving past this house on a near nightly basis.

He lights a cigarette, inhales, and looks at the digital clock on the car radio: 12:14 am. He cracks the window and waits.

At 12:17 a pair of headlights swings into the street in front of him, approaching slowly. He leans down a little to avoid being seen, but he is far enough away, and parked on the other side of the street anyways, so he knows there's no reason to worry. The car slows, its brakes squeaking a little, and eases into the driveway. The garage door goes up to reveal a dim orange light and a myriad of things very much at home in a garage: A lawnmower, some tools hanging on the back wall, a couple garbage cans.

Burnham flicks his cigarette away and trots through the front yard as the rusty old Cavalier crawls to a stop in the garage. He leans against the siding next to the opening, listening for the sound of the driver's side door opening and then closing. When he hears the rusty *wunk* of the door slamming shut, he peeks around the corner.

A chunky Mexican woman stands with her back to him, fumbling with her keys next to the car door. Her hair stretches down her back, drooping to a few inches below her ass, like a horse's tail. She has on maroon scrubs, which answers a question for him: she must be a nurse.

He wants to say something, and nearly does, but then the door that leads into the house opens, and little Anna comes hopping out excitedly. Frank stands behind her in the doorway with a huge horse's grin on his face.

"Mommy!" the girl shouts, and Burnham's legs go rubbery at the sound of her voice. He hadn't noticed it before, back at Benny's Burgers, but Anna's voice sounds remarkably similar to Harmony's.

An odd mixture of hatred and love fills him, threatens to pull his feet out from beneath him. He reaches in his pocket and feels his lighter, the rough grooves of its spark wheel against his thumb. This calms him, brings him back to reality a little, but he can't shake the odd emotion that has overwhelmed him — a feeling that only gets worse when Frank's mother bends down and wraps her arms around the little girl in a tight, motherly embrace.

25

It suddenly occurs to Burnham that he isn't sure what he's doing here, what the point of this visit is. He's been toying with the idea of vandalizing the place, maybe starting a small fire in the garage, but now he's just confused… and thankful that he hadn't spoken when he saw Frank's mother exiting her car. What would he have said? What would've been the point?

As she walks into the house, Frank's mother presses a button on the wall and the garage door begins to rumble shut. Burnham scampers down the driveway but stops when he sees a newspaper lying at the foot of the curb. His hands begin to shake and then he laughs under his breath. He plucks up the newspaper, unrolls it, sets it aflame with his lighter, and pushes it into Frank's mailbox.

Burnham sprints to his car and drives off, laughing uncontrollably all the way home.

*

Harmony hops off her purple bicycle, points at the candy store a couple doors down, and says, "I want some! Can we? Please, Bernie?"

Burnham stops and stands up, his feet on either side of his Huffy bike.

It's a bright yellow day with blue skies and

wispy, tissue-thin clouds scattered about like white freckles. The wind is like nestling your cheek against freshly dried towels.

"Okay," Burnham tells her. "But I only have two dollars. One candy for you, one for me."

She hops up and down, her sandy blonde pigtails bouncing. Her hair sparkles in the sunshine.

"Yay! Thanks, Bernie! You're the best big brother *EVER*!"

He smiles and hands her the two dollars. There are a few people wandering the sidewalks, and a few cars cruising up and down Main Street, but it's not too busy in town today. Burnham recognizes many of the people as neighbors and other common townsfolk. There's really nothing to be nervous about, and anyways, he doesn't feel like taking the time to chain their bikes to the bike rack.

"Okay, Harmony," he says, "I'll stay here and watch our bikes. You can go in the candy store by yourself, but you have to come back the second you're done. Got it?"

She nods her head emphatically. "Yes, of course, of course, I will."

Harmony giggles and scampers away.

Burnham watches her disappear into the front door, turns his head to watch the moderate town traffic drift by, leans against the brick wall of Ed's Hardware, and pulls a cigarette to lips. He'd stolen a couple packs from Sammy's Quick Stop a few days ago, which was fine, no one would miss them. But, of course, Harmony had found them stashed way in his bedroom and confronted him about it. He'd been somewhat embarrassed about it, but he was more afraid that she'd tell on him. So instead of panicking and snapping at her, which would be an open invitation to go narcing to Mom, he sat down with her and had a friendly chat. He explained to her that since he was underage, he had stolen the cigarettes when the cashier wasn't behind the counter where they were kept. He also explained that it was wrong to steal and that he regretted it and hoped to never have to do it again, which was the truth (his friend Tony was turning eighteen soon, so stealing wouldn't be necessary anymore). Burnham told Harmony that he trusted her and she liked that. Then she promised not to tattle on him. Problem solved. And still, even today, Burnham feels the need to be overly nice to her, to let her have her way — and it seems like she knows it. She's acting cheery, but she keeps asking for stuff, seemingly manipulating him in her own childish way to let her have whatever she wants.

He lights the cigarette now, inhales quickly, and then cradles the cigarette in his palm, hiding it from plain view so he won't be caught. Burnham is much more careful now. If a little girl could catch him in the act, then a cop definitely could, if he wasn't extremely careful.

A minute or so after he stomps out the cigarette, Harmony comes sprinting out of the candy store, a wild and determined look on her face. She appears to be cradling something.

"What's the big rush?" he asks her.

She says, "Quick, quick, let's go!"

As she approaches Burnham notices what it is she's cradling against her chest: about fourteen Snickers bars. He grabs her arm and says, "What are you doing with all those?"

"Let go, Bernie, let *go*!"

He pulls her away from her bike. "Did you steal these? You little *thief*! What did I tell you about stealing?"

She makes a mean and angry face, a sharp scowl that is, in its own way, quite cute. "If you can steal, *I* can steal!"

He sighs and kneels down in front of her. He looks back towards the candy store, but no one has followed her. He has to admit, he's a little impressed that she could get away with it. Hiding this odd feeling of pride, he says, "Yes, but I told you, I regret stealing because it makes me feel like a *bad* guy, like in the movies. You know how in the movies the bad guys always steal, and the good guys always do the right thing? I learned it the hard way, but I definitely would rather be a good guy than a bad guy. I want to do the *right* thing, and the right thing to do now would be to return the candy bars and apologize."

Harmony drops the Snickers bars to the ground, places her hands on her hips, and shakes her head. "Nuh-uh, no way. *You* do it!"

Burnham points at the candy bars. "Pick them up. *Now*."

"No."

"You got yourself in trouble. No one's gonna save you. You have to do it yourself. Consider it a lesson. Trust me, you'll be glad after you give them back. You'll feel a lot better."

"If you don't do it, I'll tell Mom you stole cigarettes and that I saw you smoking."

"Okay, that's fine. Mom will be mad at me for sure, but I'm a teenager. She'll be *way* more disappointed when she finds out *you* stole candy. So if you wanna play this game, that's fine. I'm willing to take the fall because Mom will be more focused on her little girl turning into a little thief."

This finally seems to get through to her. Harmony thinks it over, toeing at the ground beneath her and at the pile of candy bars. Then she sticks her tongue out at him, bends over, and begins scooping the Snickers bars up. Burnham smiles and helps her pile them against her chest, as they were before.

She looks up at him and says, "You're mean," and then walks slowly back to the candy store.

Burnham turns away and lights a second cigarette. By the time he finishes it, it occurs to him that Harmony is taking too long. It *is* a candy store, and a child can get lost in her excitement in such a place, but Harmony isn't in there shopping right now. Maybe the cashier is lecturing her, which could be a good thing, but if it goes on as long as this, in Burnham's eyes, that's just overdoing it. Harmony's a little girl. She can only take so much berating. Maybe he should go in and help her out.

Burnham stamps out the cigarette, wheels

both bikes to the rack, and chains them both up. He makes the short trek to the candy store, but then freezes before going in. There on the ground, a couple feet from the curb, are three unopened Snickers bars. Burnham's heart thuds as he turns and pulls the candy store's door open. He looks around. There are a few folks shopping, but not many. It doesn't take long for him to notice that Harmony isn't here.

A couple hours later, she is registered as missing.

Two weeks later, she is declared dead.

*

Burnham hoists his mother from the wheelchair and lays her atop the bed. She lets out a soft grunt as she tries to adjust her position. Burnham helps her slip the pillow beneath her head.

He looks her over. Her hair is whiter than it should be for a woman of fifty-five, but there is a certain beauty in it, too. It still seems lively, bouncy, as if it's in some sort of denial, clinging to whatever life it has left.

There are thick bags beneath her eyes and pink blotches here and there on her cheeks. Her lips are thin and pale. Burnham can almost see the skull beneath her face, but at the same time there is still something mysteriously youthful about her. If he stares at her long enough, he can almost see Harmony in there.

"When your sister died — " his mother begins, but he interrupts her.

"Don't, Mom. It's time for sleep."

She continues anyways. "When she died, it wasn't your fault. I'm sorry if I was distant, but I hope you know it wasn't your fault."

Burnham takes a deep breath and smiles at her, hoping she can't see in his eyes what this revelation means to him. She's said it before, quite a few times, but not since she's been sick. He isn't quite sure how to feel about it. On one hand, he's grateful for her moment of clarity here, and it touches him to know she worries about him, even in her current state. He also knows there's a place deep within him that needs to hear that Harmony's disappearance wasn't his fault, but there's another part of him that actually wishes his mother would blame him, wishes that she'd hate him with an intense vigor.

He pulls the covers up for her, nestling them under her chin. With some effort, she rolls onto her side. She smiles very subtly, comfortably.

"Do you think maybe I'm already sleeping?"

"Shh, Mom. It's okay."

Burnham reaches over and clicks the light off. The light from the hallway still illuminates her face.

"Sometimes I think I must be asleep and that when I go to bed maybe I'll *really* wake up, and I'll roll over, and your dad will be right here next to me, and maybe even Harmony will be asleep in between us."

Burnham says, "That sounds great, Mom. Sounds a lot like heaven."

Burnham was just nine — Harmony an infant — when their father died. He had been working in the yard and inexplicably collapsed. He was posthumously diagnosed with a heart murmur, a relatively minor condition that, in rare cases only, causes sudden death. Burnham's father was dead before he hit the ground. Nobody's fault.

Harmony, on the other hand…. Well, that was Burnham's fault.

Burnham's fault in part, that is, because, as much as he'd like to shoulder all the blame himself, he knows most of the blame is reserved for the kidnapper: A middle-aged man named

Rolando Flores who had, before escaping to the United States, killed five young girls in Mexico. Now, sixteen years after Harmony disappeared without a trace, Flores, convicted, is serving six consecutive life sentences in a Michigan prison.

Flores could have had his sentence reduced (as if it mattered) if he'd only revealed where Harmony's body was. But he never did. All he'd said was that he'd thrown her into a furnace.

"Heaven," Burnham's mother says through a yawn. "That sounds nice."

Burnham leaves her bedroom and begins to pull the door shut before pausing. He stares at her and listens to her rhythmic breathing. He wonders how many breaths she has left.

"Cards tomorrow," she says, her voice low and thick.

He's been living with her for two years, since her diagnosis. He'd quit his job as a news cameraman in Ohio to return to Michigan, because there was no one else alive to take care of her. And since there is some money put away — but not enough to make him rich — from the insurance payout after his father's death, Burnham is able to survive on a part-time gig as a fast food cook. This also affords him plenty of time to take care of his mother.

35

She begins humming that familiar tune again, and like before, Burnham is unable to decipher the song — but he hums along with her, remembering the melody just fine.

After a few seconds her face goes slack and she drifts off. She is beautiful when she sleeps.

"Please don't wake up," he whispers to her, and closes the door softly.

*

His sleep is a restless one, haunted by a recurring dream....

There are ribbons of black smoke and stalagmites of fire spiraling up into the sky. There are white ashes flitting around in the air like giant snowflakes. Everything is peaceful. So peaceful.

Burnham finds himself surrounded by walls of flames that, for the most part, burn quietly. He is standing in Frank's front yard and he is listening, listening. He is waiting for the sound of voices, the sound of screaming, the refreshing sound of melting.

Burnham once read on some message board that skin begins to melt around two-hundred degrees Fahrenheit. He doesn't know if it's true. But he hopes to find out.

The flames pop and crackle, like Rice Krispies. They flick high into the air, twelve, fifteen feet. They engulf everything: Frank's house, his mother's Cavalier, the tall maple tree. Leaves float down, ignite, and fold in on themselves, disappearing into glowing embers.

Burnham realizes he is holding someone's hand. He looks down, over, and sees a little girl's face. He sees the smile of angels, hears the innocent giggle. The bouncy pigtails. The squinted eyes, coffee-brown like her mother's.

Her lips move, but no sound escapes her. He reads her lips: "Hi, Bernie."

"Hey, punk," he says back, though no sound escapes him either.

Harmony looks away from him and stares into the wall of flames. A lost look creeps into her gaze. A lost, frightened look. Her eyes gleam orange.

Burnham squeezes her hand gently, thinking, *I'm here, I'll always be here*, and *I'm so sorry I made you go in alone*.

But then the light grows brighter, and the air gets uncomfortably hot and thick, and everything smells of charred wood and burnt meat. And as he tries to pull her closer to him, to protect her, she begins to drift away, somehow escaping his grip. The ground seems to liquefy and she floats, floats away from him, drifting into danger like a crippled boat on stormy seas.

She turns to face him, splashing impossibly in the grass and dirt, screaming inaudibly, tears tracking down her face. Burnham reaches, reaches, but he's rooted in, can't move, and then it happens: the terrible and glorious melting.

"Never again! Never, ever again!" he mouths, promising something he can't guarantee, can't because he knows it's hopeless, he is who he is, but *Oh God* he wants to change because there is good in him, he's not a monster, and it's just not worth it....

The walls close in and it feels like glass shattering around him, razor shards pelting his skin, and it's fire, just fire, but it's *alive*, and like all living things it needs to eat....

And oh, Jesus, the pain.

*

Burnham stands on the sidewalk and stares at the last door his sister ever opened.

The candy store closed down a few years ago and has since been replaced by a pet food store. At this hour, all the businesses on the

38

Main Street strip are closed — and anyways, the town is not as upbeat or welcoming as it was just sixteen years ago. The town is dirtier, more unsafe, more ominous. At 2:00 am, there is very little traffic.

The mid-October air is cool enough now so that Burnham can see his breath under the orange streetlamp. He stares through this white steam at the door and replays the memory of pulling it open and stepping inside only to find...nothing. He thinks about the Snickers bars lying at the curb. He'd turned his back to smoke, taken his eyes off of her, and somewhere in the five seconds it would've taken her to walk back into the candy store, Rolando Flores had pulled up to the curb and yanked her into his vehicle, into a hell that Burnham cannot possibly imagine or fathom.

He lifts a smoke to his lips and pauses before lighting it. He laughs quietly.

"But time, goes by, so slowly..." he sings softly.

"Unchained Melody." Wow, Mom, that's beautiful.

He lights the cigarette and takes a puff. He glares at the building again and flicks the lighter's wheel a few times: *snik, snik, snik....*

39

The smoke warms him, fills all the hollow places that exist deep inside of him.

He flicks the lighter again, stares at the blue eye at the base of the flame. He holds it to his cheek and fights the urge to pull away. Against excruciating pain, he counts the seconds. After twenty-one, an odd coldness spreads across his face and everything glows red out of the corner of his eye.

The Name

)—————————————(

Zilbon wrote a story when he was nineteen. It was about a young boy named Zilbon. More specifically, it was about living with a name like "Zilbon." It was a work of fiction, but some people thought it was this weird thing called "creative nonfiction" because the author had used his real name. But Zilbon worked on the story for about a week under the assumption that it was a work of fiction. He didn't try very hard, either. He wasn't a writer. The story wasn't supposed to be good because Zilbon had never written one before that. At least not outside of school. It was about 3,000 words long, and it was good, to everyone except Zilbon.

He wrote in metaphors, or symbols, or whatever the hell you call them. There was that memorable scene about his face being washed in blood, a sink full of thick, purplish blood, and he dipped his face in it like they do when you want a flavor shell around your soft serve ice cream. Zilbon was trying to capture what it felt like to live with such a strange name, to be alone in the world, to be, in some way, unrecognizable. But that was all bullshit.

In all honesty, Zilbon's life wasn't that bad. His parents, William and Darlene, were nice people. They had their problems, sure, but they were normal problems, financial stuff that all middle-class folks face. William and Darlene were the hippy type, though. Zilbon was well aware that his mom and dad smoked pot sometimes, but that didn't bother him. The only thing that really bothered him was meeting people. He hated introducing himself. "Zilbon Anderson," he'd say, extending his hand in false confidence, and it never failed. People cocked their eyebrows, or smiled nervously, or laughed. They always thought it was a joke. And they never repeated his name. Zilbon was embarrassed because everyone else was embarrassed.

When he was a kid, teachers would take roll and stumble through his name, as if "Zilbon" was difficult to pronounce. Zilbon's classmates would laugh. And most of his teachers referred to him as "Mr. Anderson."

So when Zilbon wrote his story,

appropriately titled "The Name," he wanted to capture the embarrassment he always felt when people learned his name. The problem was, of course, that Zilbon wasn't a writer, so he wasn't sure how to develop a character. So he wrote about himself because he was the only character he thought he knew.

Once, when we was about twelve, he asked his parents why they'd named him Zilbon. His dad smiled and put an arm around Zilbon's shoulder. "I love you, Bon Bon," he'd said. "Your mother and I love you very much. Isn't that what matters?" And then Darlene had inexplicably burst into tears. In hindsight, a few years later, Zilbon was fairly certain that his parents had been high that day — and probably on the day they named him, too.

When Zilbon finished "The Name," he was also finishing up his sophomore year in college. He used the story as an assignment in his English 102 class because he loathed writing academic essays, or whatever the hell you call them. Professor Larsen, of course, gave Zilbon an F on the assignment, but he also encouraged Zilbon to submit the piece for publication. "This is a fantastic story, Mr. Anderson," Prof. Larsen said, and Zilbon felt like Neo in *The Matrix* because Dr. Larsen's voice sounded very much like Agent Smith's, who was Neo's arch

43

nemesis.

A few weeks later, at the end of the semester, Prof. Larsen confronted Zilbon about the story again. "Did you ever submit that story anywhere?"

Zilbon told him, "No, that would be ridiculous," but then Prof. Larsen asked if he could submit it on Zilbon's behalf, to which Zilbon responded, "Do whatever the hell you want with it."

So that's how it started. Zilbon received a C in the class, which was fine, but then he found himself in the midst of a real shit-storm. Prof. Larsen kept emailing him because the story had been accepted to numerous publications. Prof. Larsen wanted Zilbon to choose one, and kept listing the benefits of each publication in his emails. Zilbon didn't care, so he let Prof. Larsen choose, and Prof. Larsen eventually chose some magazine called *Pushcart*.

Wait, no, that's not right. "Pushcart" was the name of the prize Zilbon would win later. Anyways, I don't remember the name of the magazine "The Name" was first published in. Let's get back to the story.

"The Name" received critical acclaim. Publishers and agents tried to contact Zilbon through Prof. Larsen. At some point Zilbon got sick of checking his email every day, so he gave Prof. Larsen his phone number. It was around this time that Prof. Larsen told Zilbon to call him "Hugh," which was strange, because Zilbon had thought his name was "Scott." Anyways, Hugh started passing Zilbon's phone number around to these publishers and agents, so Zilbon started getting all these unwanted phone calls.

"Mr. Anderson?" they'd say when he answered, and he always told them his name was Zilbon, but they kept right on calling him Mr. Anderson. It was infuriating.

They always wanted to know his background. What was his education? Did he have a degree? How many publications did he have? And so on, to which Zilbon would answer, "I passed English 102 with a C. Does that count?"

Wait. I should tell you, this is how I was born. Zilbon's story was an earthquake in the literary world. Then there was that literal earthquake, the one that cracked porcelain and shook rust into the plumbing. Or maybe it wasn't literal. Either way, there was rust in the plumbing, and when Zilbon filled the sink to shave one morning, the water came out red. And so he dunked his face in, because it seemed to him that reality and fiction had clashed here, and that the rusty water was a symbol or metaphor for the bloody sink full of water in "The Name."

Zilbon smiled at his reflection, the rust particles clinging to his beard stubble, because it had finally hit him that he could write and he did write, and that his story was so good that it came to life. So there, in the back of his head, came a voice, my voice, and it said — I said — to live this life, to milk it for all it was worth. So Zilbon colored his fingertips red with his razor and smeared crimson fingerprints all over his face. We had made a blood pact with one another, and it was my becoming.

At first Zilbon fought me, but eventually he learned to love the attention. He signed a book deal shortly after he won the Pushcart Prize. That's when he changed his name to my name, because no one would ever read a realist novel written by a guy called Zilbon Anderson. They would expect the book to be science-fiction because "Zilbon" was a futuristic or alien name, and so readers would never take the book seriously. So Zilbon became me, Bob Anderson. I was alive and I could see.

There were great reds and yellows and greens all around me: blood and sunshine and ocean water, but the ocean water wasn't literal yet because I hadn't been to the ocean. But I was here, and this was my earth, and it was my playground. I typed novels and stories and never hit the Backspace key because it was just so *colorless*. It was *essential* that my fictions and my realities collided, so I lived out the most vital parts of my plots. When my characters snapped off tree branches, I snapped off tree branches. When my characters used knives, I used knives. And when my characters drank blood, I drank blood, too. It was the only way to portray the sights, smells, sounds, and tastes of my earth with true validity.

Shortly after I was born, William and Darlene asked me why I had changed my name. I wrapped my arm around William's shoulder and said, "I love you, Bill Bill. I love you and Dar Dar very much. Isn't that what matters?" And then Darlene burst into tears before I expunged the two of them from my beautiful earth.

As for Me...

Geoff is leaning back on the sofa spooning Cinnamon Toast Crunch into his mouth. He is trying to enjoy his snack while watching the Packers game, but he keeps getting distracted by the sound of Boyd and Odessa having sex upstairs. Even as Aaron Rodgers somehow eludes a linebacker and throws a magnificent touchdown pass, Geoff barely notices, flinching at the muffled, rhythmic thumping and low moans coming from his friend's room. Boyd doesn't even bother closing his bedroom door anymore, so the moans are more audible than they should be.

Geoff wipes a drip of milk away from his chin and shouts, "Jesus, guys. Really?"

"Don't be jealous," Boyd shouts back, and Geoff can't suppress a small laugh.

Boyd has been Geoff's best friend since fourth grade, and even then, despite his young age, Geoff was aware of something off about Boyd. But back then Boyd's antics were limited to harmless things, like ignoring the "Private Property" and "No Trespassing" signs on Old Lady Amelia's chain-link fence and sneaking over to pick apples off her tree. It wasn't until seventh grade that Boyd began doing truly harmful things.

"You guys are disgusting," Geoff says now, still smiling a little despite how awkward he feels. The thumping eases for a moment, followed by a sexy female giggle that actually stirs something in Geoff, makes him aware of his capability to entertain lustful thoughts.

"No, *this* bitch is disgusting," Boyd shouts. "In a good way!"

From fourth through seventh grade, Geoff and Boyd would sometimes head down to the pond behind Boyd's house to catch tadpoles in empty Miracle Whip jars. There wasn't much of a purpose to catching the tadpoles, at least not that Geoff could figure, but he enjoyed it just the same, if only because it was something to do with his buddy. After a while, however, Geoff and Boyd made a game out of it, a sort of competition to see who could capture the most tadpoles. They'd plunge the jars in, cap them off, and rush back to the picnic table in Boyd's backyard. Once there, they'd dump the contents of the jars out, carefully, so that only the water spilled off the table and not their trophies, and count as many tadpoles as they could see. It was a fun, relatively innocent game, although hundreds of tadpoles had of course lost their lives over the span of those four summers. But there was nothing malicious about it. Not then. Not until the first week of seventh grade, when Boyd took a rubber mallet to the tadpoles, joyously smashing them into a soupy goo atop the picnic table. After that Geoff couldn't quite bring himself to catch tadpoles anymore, although he had to admit there was something alluring about the violence of it all, an urge that told him to keep Boyd around for reasons his young mind couldn't quite comprehend.

After a few minutes the thumping, giggling, and moaning cease completely. Geoff, rinsing his now empty cereal bowl in the kitchen sink, shouts, "That didn't take long," and Odessa says, "Are you kidding me? That was his personal record!"

Geoff laughs and hears Boyd say to her, "You're good, baby, but I've had better in prison."

Geoff slumps into the sofa again and gazes at the TV. "Hey Boyd," he calls, "you should get down here. It's already seventeen to zip, end of the first quarter."

"Fuck the game!" Boyd says, and Odessa laughs hysterically.

"What are you guys up to?"

It's Boyd's voice again: "Our eyes in blow." Odessa laughs again, and then Geoff hears the distinct screech of a credit card sliding across glass, followed by an exaggerated sniff.

Geoff lets out a sigh, lifts the TV remote, and cranks the volume to ear-bleeding level. The Packers, on their best days, help Geoff to forget about Boyd's previous two prison sentences — both for cocaine possession. And though Boyd now claims to be sober, his definition is misguided: "I'm sober four days a week," he'd said recently, adding that he's *especially* sober every Tuesday, because he has to attend an addiction support group every Tuesday night. Just recently Geoff saw Boyd flipping his "One Year Sober" chip into the air like a coin — while watching Odessa snort a line with this distant, happy look on his face.

Sometime in the third quarter, with the Pack leading Minnesota 23-7, Geoff hears

51

stomping above him and the unmistakable sound of arguing, one voice reaching for a level of volume far above the other, and the other attempting to do the same in return. But before he can press the mute button on his TV remote to hear what Boyd and Odessa are arguing about, a terrible thumping sound startles him. He turns his head to the left to see Odessa's topless body tumbling down the stairs, her momentum stopped by the wall at the bottom of the flight. She hits the wall face first, her head bending awkwardly up and to the left, and rolls over onto her right side, unconscious. Geoff, seated on the sofa just a few feet away, glares wide-eyed at the sight of her bloodied face; Odessa's nose is quite obviously broken, and blood runs from the corner of her pink mouth, as well, collecting in a tiny crimson circle on the beige linoleum. But what really catches Geoff's attention is Odessa's blue eyes, those sparkling gems that capture him and fill him with jealousy. Her eyes are open, and she isn't moving.

"What the fuck?" Geoff says, getting to his feet.

Boyd, wearing nothing but boxer shorts, appears on the stairs about halfway down. There's the faintest indication of white powder on his chest, caked into the sweat beads above his pectoral muscles. He's staring at Odessa with a disinterested, somewhat expectant look on his face, as if he's waiting for Geoff to mop the blood off the floor. Boyd is holding an old black revolver, and for a moment Geoff thinks his friend is about to shoot him, but then Boyd says, "I pushed her. I just pushed the bitch."

"What? Why?"

"I…. Geoff, I want to tell you I didn't mean it, but I did. I fucking killed that bitch."

Geoff just stares at Odessa's chest, her large, dark nipples, and he realizes that she isn't breathing. Part of him is glad to receive such a gift as the sight of her exposed breasts, but the better part of him says, *Jesus, man, this is no time for sexual thoughts.*

"I'm not going back to prison," Boyd says. "Can't." The revolver shakes in his right hand, but other than that, nothing about Boyd's body language indicates he's nervous or upset.

"Jesus Christ, man. Jesus *Christ.*"

"Even if we said it was an accident they'd figure me out somehow. I could flush the coke or something, but my head's in the clouds right now. Can't hide it."

Boyd has spent nearly eight of the last nine years serving time for cocaine possession. He's

53

already been in twice. Three strikes, you're out: *Sorry, kids, Boyd can't come out to play today. He's serving a life term for drug possession and manslaughter.*

Geoff kneels down and touches his fingers to Odessa's wrist, where his elementary teacher had taught him to look for a pulse some twenty years ago. Geoff has felt his own pulse hundreds of times over the years, fascinated by the rhythmic pressure against his fingers. This is the first time he's been unable to feel anything. It occurs to him that Odessa is no longer a person. In a split second she has become an object.

"You've been together for a year," Geoff says. "You've been out for a year, Boyd. Jesus, man. Your life's getting on track."

"She threw a handful of coke at me and I just saw red. Fuck me. *Fuck* me. I loved her, Geoff. I did, I really did." Boyd inches down the steps slowly, the revolver dangling at his side.

"What's the gun for?"

Boyd smiles a little, like a little kid who just got caught saying a swear. "You'll think I'm crazy. Please don't think I'm crazy. But after I pushed her and I saw her rolling down the stairs like that I knew…that if she lived, I'd have to finish the job." Boyd makes eye contact with

Geoff, his brow furrowed, dark eyes serious. "I'm not going back. No way, Geoff. No fucking way."

Geoff's mind drifts to seventh grade. The pond. The jars. The pendulum motion of the mallet. The jelly-like soup atop the picnic table. Boyd's smile. His laughter.

"What's that, a warning?" Geoff says. "Screw you, Boyd. You aren't even supposed to own a gun. Is that thing legal?"

"Is anything I do legal?" Boyd laughs.

Geoff shakes his head and runs his hands through his hair. He lets out a worried puff of air and thinks, *I need a cigarette.*

Boyd takes another step down and says, "We have to move it. The body."

"Where? I mean…my God…this *can't* be happening."

"It's almost dark. Let's just wait a few minutes. I'll get dressed and then we'll load it into your trunk and drive it out to my mom's place. We can drop it in the pond. Or bury it out there in the woods."

Geoff forces Odessa's eyes closed and stands up. He looks away, back to the football game. The Packers are ahead 30-7 now. Small victories.

"The pond's frozen over by now," Geoff says. "And the ground will be too hard to dig up. And what if your mom sees us? Plus I'm not sure I'm comfortable driving three hours with a body in my trunk. It's too risky."

"She won't see us. She won't."

Geoff turns around again. Boyd is starting to get antsy. He's wavering on the steps a bit, glaring at Geoff with a frustrated expression. The gun, dull and black, is still aimed at the floor, but Boyd seems to have a tighter grip now. And his index finger is curled around the trigger.

Geoff says, "Okay. Okay. Fine. I'll help you. *Fuck me*, Boyd, I'll help you, but only because you're making me nervous."

"Nervous?"

"Who knows what goes on in that poisoned head of yours, Boyd. Does anything about this situation *not* make you nervous?" Boyd just shrugs and glances at Odessa again. "Go get dressed," Geoff says.

"She's got great tits, doesn't she?"

"Go get dressed."

56

*

Geoff has worked hard to put his life together. Since Boyd has spent so much time in prison, Geoff feels as if he missed out on his twenties, especially since he opted to spend his time apart from his best friend building a future. Geoff has sacrificed a personal life, instead spending his time saving money and moving up the ladder at Gary's Furniture, which has recently expanded to include three other locations in Michigan. Geoff is now the area manager at the St. Ignace location, just north of the Mackinaw Bridge.

Instead of worrying about dating, which costs money and usually doesn't pan out, or going to local pubs to sing karaoke and waste his savings on beer and shots, Geoff has focused on his career. He tries to keep in touch with his parents and his sister, who still live on the west side of Michigan's Upper Peninsula, and he has a few coworkers he considers friends, but Geoff's life is all about earning money in peace. He spends most of his free time working out, cooking, watching the Packers, and writing. Geoff knows he's not a very good writer, but he enjoys putting stories together, the feeling he gets when he composes a particularly violent piece about a serial killer or a rapist. He wonders where such thoughts originate, since he isn't a particularly violent man — he's never hurt anyone before, or killed an animal with malicious intent — but the ideas that drive his writing are almost always controversial and disturbing, and bloody. This gives him a thrill and reminds him that there are untapped parts of his own consciousness, areas of his psyche that even he may never fully understand.

After Boyd's first prison term expired seven years ago, Geoff was quick to take him into his apartment, which was located within reasonable driving distance of both Boyd's mother and Geoff's family, long before he earned his promotion and moved to St. Ignace. Boyd had only served a year, but the two of them were still only twenty-two, and there was a primal part of Geoff that wanted very badly to have a night life, to drink and smoke and get in a little bit of trouble, maybe a bar fight or two. And anyways, up until that point, Geoff hadn't been apart from his buddy for more than a few weeks at a time. Yes, Geoff visited Boyd in jail a few times, but it wasn't the same; they simply couldn't hang out, and it was weird and scary with all the eyes staring at them, from other convicts and prison guards alike. Everyone watched Geoff suspiciously, as if he were going to try and break Boyd out, as if he were going to sneak in a cake with a file baked into it, like you'd see on a Bugs Bunny cartoon.

But Boyd hadn't bothered with the addiction support group assigned to him then, or made any effort to get a job. He instantly fell back into his old ways and got arrested again within a couple of months, when he unintentionally overdosed in the bathroom of a local bar. Geoff still thinks about seeing his friend in the hospital, the sunken look of his eyes and his pallid skin. He thinks about the helplessness, how he had tried to help Boyd get his life together and how he'd ultimately failed, how nothing he could have done would've made a real difference back then. But times are different now. Boyd is different. He's made an effort — a small one, yes, but it's a step in the right direction. He's even held a girlfriend for a year and earned a job at the Hot Dog Hut. Not to mention the fact that he's been attending his Tuesday night support groups.

And now this. A bad snap decision. People will call it murder if Boyd is caught. But Boyd is not a murderer. A junkie, yes. Maybe even a bad person. But he's not a murderer. Geoff knows him. He knows his buddy better than he knows anyone, maybe even better than he knows himself. It's for this reason that Geoff is willing to put his own well-being at risk, *because — let's face it — you'll go to prison this time, too.*

59

Geoff drives his car west along US-2, navigating through Manistique and Escanaba before arriving in their old hometown of Iron Mountain, some three-and-a-half hours from Geoff's very safe and peaceful life in Saint Ignace. Though it is December and some snows have fallen already, they've lucked out tonight: the winter storm that was supposed to pass through has, according to the weatherman on the radio, missed them to the north. The roads are in perfect driving condition. The only hiccup has been Boyd's silent hysterics, the way his eyes keep darting around, the way he keeps talking about Odessa's body in the trunk, the way he waves the gun around when he talks, and the fact that he refuses to wear a seatbelt. But, Geoff has to admit, Boyd has become very good at being high; he doesn't bounce off the walls like some cocaine addicts, and he isn't very talkative. The cocaine, it seems, calms him. And fills him with murderous rage, too.

As Geoff eases onto Boyd's old street — the dirt road his mother still lives on — Boyd says, "Turn the lights off. She might see."

Geoff says, "She won't," but flicks the lights off anyways, cringing as the old Impala's struts squeak over the road's washboard-like surface.

After a quarter-mile or so, Geoff takes a

60

right into the first driveway — not the second one, which leads to the house, but the snowy, unplowed drive that leads to the back of the property, out by the rickety old barn and beyond that, the pond, both of which are a couple hundred yards or more from the house. Fortunately, Boyd's old house is a good half-mile from the nearest neighbor's, and there's nothing across the road but dense, skeletal forest that creeps up almost to the shoulder. It's unlikely they'll be seen.

But someone'll see the tire tracks tomorrow, Geoff thinks.

"Watch the brake lights," Boyd says as the car crawls nearer to the barn.

The barn used to be one of Boyd and Geoff's favorite hangouts. It had lain empty since Boyd's father died (he'd been killed in a car accident a few years before Geoff and Boyd met), but before that, according to Boyd, his father kept a combine parked inside. Boyd's father had farmed the plot of land to the west of the house, the empty field that is now overgrown with weeds and bushes, further obscuring them from the neighbor's house on the other side.

Boyd's mother had sold the combine after her husband was killed, leaving the barn empty,

61

except for the spiders, skunks, and other critters that would take refuge for a little while. Geoff and Boyd, in fifth grade, started coming here to smoke Boyd's mother's cigarettes, or to play hide-and-seek in the unused horse stables.

Geoff circles the car around so the brake lights face away from the house, and comes to a stop. He kills the engine, meets his friend's gaze, and then steps out. The car's engine parts clink softly as it cools down.

"Been a long time," Boyd says, and it occurs to Geoff that Boyd probably hasn't talked to his mother in many years. She had all but disowned him after his second arrest, but Boyd has talked so little of her that Geoff had all but forgotten about their strained relationship.

The sight of the barn in the cool moonlight fills Geoff with a comfortable nostalgia. It doesn't look much different from the last time he saw it, some eight years ago, but he's willing to bet that in the daylight it's more brown than red these days. Snow has drifted up against the barn's flank, a reminder that northern Michigan's winters are nothing to fuck with, but tonight the sky is clear and starry, the air calm and silent. It's also incredibly cold — the Impala's digital temperature indicator had dropped from eleven degrees Fahrenheit to just two degrees by the time they arrived.

"What now?" Geoff asks.

"My dad's shovels might still be in the barn."

The knob on the side door is loose and rattles, but with a bit of effort Boyd is able to force the door open. The interior of the barn smells of oil and hay, but even in the darkness Geoff can tell it's quite empty in here.

Boyd flicks a switch and two dim bulbs, no more than 75 watts each, cast an orange glow atop the ground, which is just hardened sand. Up above, a third bulb shines in the hayloft, but it's so distant it doesn't help.

Old oil quarts line the shelves that are nailed to the east wall to their right. A Clorox bottle with its top cut off appears to be full of a blackish fluid, maybe used oil, maybe something else. A relatively new-looking Craftsman lawn tractor is parked beneath the shelves, along with a push mower that appears to have been bought in the 1970s and a gas powered weed whacker. A collection of rakes and shovels hang from the north wall. Other than these few items, the place is quite desolate.

"Doesn't look like Mom uses this much."

"Enough to change the lightbulbs."

Geoff and Boyd each carry a shovel outside and jab them into the snow-covered ground near the Impala. It takes some effort to push them into the frozen ground.

"This is gonna be a bitch," Boyd says.

Geoff is quite aware of the dead body in his car's trunk, but he's feeling rather calm at this point. The drive here had been stressful, but from this point on it'll be smooth sailing — no way they'll be caught now, no need to worry about getting pulled over by some bored cop, or Odessa miraculously waking up and somehow escaping the vehicle, or Boyd flipping his top and blowing both of their brains out.

There is a chance, of course, that someone — probably Boyd's mother — will find the body someday, and when that happens, well, it'll be over for both of them. Not to mention that Odessa will be reported missing very soon, with her last known whereabouts being Geoff's house. On the ride over, Boyd had mentioned that because Odessa always walks from her apartment to Geoff's place — a distance of a mile or so, not much more — it's quite possible she could get abducted on her way home, and Geoff had agreed that that would be their story when the cops came knocking. Geoff also realizes that because Boyd already has a record, he will be the one implicated in Odessa's disappearance, at least at first. Boyd may or may not be able to get them off his tail, but Geoff is confident that he (Geoff) can play dumb and avoid suspicion. After all, Geoff has never done anything to warrant suspicion.

For a moment Geoff considers trying to convince Boyd to take the body somewhere else — it seems quite stupid to bury your girlfriend's body at your mom's house — but this might be the nail in Boyd's coffin, the very thing that eliminates Geoff as a suspect. The police might, of course, consider that Geoff had helped Boyd, and perhaps that he had even driven the transport vehicle (he has, after all), but they'd never be able to prove it, and Geoff is, in his own eyes, a good liar. Boyd may even fess up to the cops, tell them everything, including how Geoff had helped dig the grave, but it would be a "his word versus mine" kind of situation. Geoff realizes that he's never had to create a lie as big as this one before, but he is confident in his ability to save his own ass.

"Let's get to it then," Geoff says and moves forward to open the trunk of the Impala. As he slides the key in, however, he stops, listening. There's a muffled musical chiming coming from inside the car.

"What's that?" Geoff asks. "Your phone?"

Boyd says, "Nope, not mine. I always keep it on silent."

Then, with a heavy dread settling over him, Geoff realizes it must be Odessa's cellphone. She's topless, yes, but she *is* wearing shorts. Her phone must be in one of the pockets. *Odessa isn't dead, after all, but she is trapped in the trunk. She made a phone call. She called for help, and now they're calling back to check on her.*

Though the air is bitterly cold, heat rises in Geoff's cheeks and sweat breaks out on his forehead. He turns the key and the trunk opens with a hollow *thunk*. The musical chiming grows louder. Grimly, expecting to see Odessa's terrified eyes staring at him, Geoff peers inside.

But she is dead. Of course. She is as unmoving and lifeless as the night wind.

Boyd suddenly plunges his hand into Odessa's shorts pocket and withdraws her phone. "It's her sister," he says, looking at the touchscreen face.

"Let it go to voicemail," Geoff says.

Boyd glances at him, smiles, and accepts the call. Geoff's heart sinks and a sickness rises in him. For one horrific moment he is sure Boyd is about to confess, but then Boyd says, "Dallas, always the worrier, always gotta play the part of big sister. Odessa's fine. *Everyone's* fine."

Geoff takes a relieved breath of air.

"No need," Boyd says into the phone. "Asleep…. I would, but she's asleep…. Yeah, *dead* tired." Boyd winks at Geoff. "No, we're fine, staying out of trouble. I'm watching *Sportscenter* with Geoff…. Come on, now, give me more credit than that!"

Though he doesn't own a watch, Geoff taps his wrist, indicating to Boyd that they're wasting time. Boyd puts a finger up: *one minute*.

"No, no, don't come over…Yeah, Geoff's not feeling that great…Flu, I think. The shit flu…. Odessa doesn't need a ride…Yeah, she can walk like always. She'll be fine. It's only like a mile…. I'm serious, Dallas, don't come over…Well, yeah, but it's more than that. Geoff just doesn't wanna see you…Yes, Odessa's fine. We're all fine…Sure thing, big sis…Sure thing. Goodnight."

As Boyd, smiling like a jackass, touches the cellphone's screen to end the call, Geoff says,

"You're out of your goddamn mind. What were you thinking?"

"Ease up, man. I'm just having a little fun."

"Fun? This is *fun* to you? Killing your girlfriend is your idea of a good time?"

Boyd's smile fades and something sinister rises in his dark eyes. His face goes slack. Even in the moonlight, Geoff can sense a terrible change in his friend. He can sense Boyd's instability, how his mood can change on a dime. Geoff realizes that, most likely, murdering Odessa has awakened something in Boyd, some kind of monster. He realizes, with a feeling somewhere between dread and thrill, that this probably won't be the last time Boyd kills. And just as this thought crosses Geoff's mind, Boyd confirms it when he says, "Mom's next."

"What?"

"As soon as we're done here. We're going up to the house. We're gonna knock on the door. She'll wake up and invite us in, I'm sure, and then I'm gonna slit her backstabbing throat." There is an ominous finality in his voice.

Geoff, hovering over Odessa's body, stares at him for a few seconds. Boyd's face is serious, but then he lifts the corners of his mouth again, this time in an obviously fake smile.

"You're with me, right Geoff?"

Geoff, aware now of how dangerous his friend really is, tries not to hesitate. It would be bad news to appear reluctant at this point. "I put a roof over your head, didn't I?"

Boyd laughs. "That you did, my man. Out of everyone in my whole pathetic life, you're the only person who never did me wrong."

"You're my friend."

Boyd leans on his shovel and glances towards the pond. "A lot of memories here, huh?"

"Good memories," Geoff says, and he means it. Some part of him wishes he could drift back in time, not just to a few hours ago to prevent Odessa's death — she was smoking hot, but Geoff didn't much care about her — but to years ago, before Boyd ever lifted a rubber mallet. The stress of tonight has reached its boiling point, and Geoff longs for a feeling of peace again. He wants to veg out on his sofa watching a Packers game. He wants to pop his ear buds in and take a jog in the local park. He wants to sit down, light a smoke, and begin writing a novel. He wants to go home, back to his quiet,

69

reclusive life in St. Ignace, before Boyd moved in.

Before they begin the arduous task of lifting Odessa's body out of the trunk (getting her in wasn't so bad, but it's true, Geoff thinks, what they say about dead weight being a bitch to lift), Boyd leans in and kisses her forehead. It would be a touching moment if Boyd hadn't impulsively murdered her a few hours ago. Then he moves lower and kisses her breasts, and Geoff has to look away to avoid getting sick.

When Boyd stands up he looks at Geoff and says, "Wanna give her a kiss goodnight?" Geoff shakes his head quickly and Boyd says, "I wouldn't mind, you know," as if the reason Geoff won't do it is because he's afraid of offending Boyd.

"I know," Geoff says. "Let's just get this over with."

"Should we dig the hole first?"

Geoff shrugs. "I don't think it matters," he says, hiding the fact that he just wants the body of out his car.

They begin lifting Odessa out, Geoff handling her head and shoulders. Her head keeps lolling around, the neck having been broken in the fall. It's like a bowling ball in a sock attached to a human body. With some effort, though she weighs no more than 130 pounds, they heave her out, Geoff losing his grip and dropping her upper body to the ground. Boyd just laughs and tosses the legs aside the way you'd toss dirty laundry.

"We can do better than that," Boyd says, and moves to take hold of Odessa's upper body. Geoff gives him a wide berth, maneuvering around to the feet.

They lift her up and move towards the pine forest, just behind the tiny pond. The forest here isn't too dense, so they're not struggling to push branches aside or shield their faces. Geoff notices that the air feels a bit warmer, and there is very little snow on the forest floor. It might be easier to dig in here, though the ground is surely almost as frozen as outside. At least they won't have to worry about digging through the three or four inches of crunchy old snow that fell days ago.

They drop Odessa's body atop a gathering of brown pine needles and it occurs to Geoff that he could end this madness. It hits him that he's an accomplice in murder and doesn't that, in some way, make him a murderer, too? He has Boyd's trust. He could use that to gain the upper

71

hand. He could take a shovel upside Boyd's drug-poisoned head, call the cops, and claim Boyd had held him at gunpoint, forced him to drive here and help him dispose of the body. It's a perfectly reasonable explanation. If Geoff could manage to turn on some waterworks there's no way he'd be implicated — no way anyone would know that he'd actually volunteered to assist Boyd. Doing this wouldn't save Odessa's life, of course, but it would save his own, as well as Boyd's mother's. Then Geoff could simply ease back into his old, quiet, perfectly insignificant life.

After they retrieve the shovels, Geoff and Boyd return to the forest and begin stabbing them into the solid ground. It takes a good amount of effort to penetrate the surface and neither of them are able to remove more than just a few inches of dirt at a time, but they are making progress. They agree not to go deeper than four feet or so, since that will take too long, and anyways, why is it such a universal rule that graves are dug to a depth of six feet? What difference would that extra two feet make? And Geoff wonders just how deep they'll get before the ground becomes too hard to dig into anymore, since they're bound to hit frozen clay at any time.

But before he can find out, a female voice

72

startles him: "What's going on out here?"

Geoff and Boyd spin around, and though it is quite dark in the pine forest, Geoff can make out a medium-height, rather rotund figure a few feet away.

Boyd, surprise in his voice, says, "Mom?"

"Boyd? What the hell are you doing?"

There is a second of silence that seems to stretch out forever, and Geoff thinks, *This is it. The defining moment of our lives.*

"So many distractions," Boyd says, his voice barely audible, as if he's speaking to himself. He's also clearly agitated, which could be a sign that he's about to lash out.

"Are you doing drugs? Are you two out here getting high? What are you doing here?"

Geoff answers quickly, before Boyd can react: "Yes, Mrs. Renfro. We buried it out here a long time ago, and we just came back to get it." Boyd laughs a little, a menacing sound that seems to say, *Good one, Geoff.*

Mrs. Renfro's voice drops. "Get the hell off my property."

"Mom, it's — "

73

"Get out of here before I call the police. I never want to see you again. Both of you."

Geoff cringes, hurt. He knows he deserves her scorn, but he likes and respects her. She was always nice, if a little quiet and strange at times. Sometimes she would sit unmoving and stare out the window for minutes on end, as if she were a robot and someone had flicked her off switch. Geoff supposed it had a lot to do with Mr. Renfro's death. Boyd had told Geoff some time back that the car had burned up, cooking Mr. Renfro alive. Geoff knows he'd be messed up, too. He never blamed her, and anyways, even though she was weird, she never said or did anything to frighten or anger Geoff.

"Fine," Boyd says, his voice calm, eerie. "You've been kicking me out ever since Dad died. This one last time won't bother me."

"Get off my property," she says again, and Geoff can see she's raised a hand, pointing a finger in the direction of the car.

Boyd sighs and lowers his head. He moves forward, the shovel dangling at his right side. Geoff, uneasy, follows him, watching him closely. There's an intense moment as Boyd shuffles past his mother, a split second when Geoff is sure Boyd will raise the shovel and bring it down on her head, caving it in like a melon. Geoff, both hands on his own shovel, tightens his grip, but then loosens it again and lets out a long, relieved wisp of breath as Boyd continues on quietly. Geoff, no longer tense, turns his attention to Mrs. Renfro and offers her a friendly smile and a nod of his head as he approaches her. She doesn't respond, only stares at him with a sort of tired disappointment in her eyes, as if to say, *I expected better of you.*

But as he moves next to her, Geoff senses movement in front of him and looks up just in time to see Boyd charging, the shovel pulled back over his head like a sledgehammer.

Geoff, surprised, throws his hands up and waves his arms. "Wait! Stop, stop!"

Boyd halts in his tracks with a confused expression. "What? *Stop*?" The shovel is still over his head, and judging by his facial expression, he seems, in some way, to be almost asking Geoff for permission to continue, waiting for the go-ahead to bring the shovel's metal head down on his mother's skull.

Mrs. Renfro turns, sees Boyd, and moves away quickly, putting Geoff between her and her son. An expression of reserved terror and confusion sweeps across her age-lined face.

"What are you *doing*? Boyd?"

"Just, everyone calm down," Geoff says, his hands up, palms out like a traffic cop urging a vehicle to stop. "Take it easy, both of you. We can all just work this thing out."

Boyd finally lowers the shovel, smiles, shrugs, and says, "There's nothing to work out, Geoff. We both know how this ends."

Mrs. Renfro, her voice trembling, says, "How *what* ends? Oh…*God*."

Geoff looks at her and says, quite harshly, "Shhh. Just be quiet for a minute."

Geoff cycles through the possible outcomes, tries to reason with himself that there's a way out of this that doesn't end with more dead bodies. No matter how he tries to fathom a reasonable end to this situation, however, he can only see two outcomes: Either Mrs. Renfro ends up dead, or she calls the cops and Geoff and Boyd go on the run. And Geoff knows almost all manhunts end in the hunted being caught. Prison doesn't sound too appealing.

But then, neither does murdering his best friend's mother.

As if reading Geoff's mind, Boyd says, "Listen, bro. If we let her go, she'll call the

76

cops, and we'll *both* go to prison. I mean, if you wanna go, that's your problem, but I already told you I'm not going back. You don't know how it is. You don't have any clue, man. Like I said, get arrested, go ahead, go to jail for the rest of your life. I don't care. As for me? No way I'm going back. No matter what."

Mrs. Renfro says, "Why are you doing this? Why would you want to hurt me? I'm your *mother*, for Christ's sake!"

Geoff, annoyed, glares at her. "I said *be quiet*!" He points at her feet. "Sit down on the ground there."

Boyd lets out a sarcastic laugh. "Bitch doesn't know *how* to be quiet."

"I know you," Mrs. Renfro says, voice cracking. She sits and crosses her legs. "You're my son, and I know you. This isn't you."

Boyd smiles at her and slowly lifts a finger to his lips. *Shhhhhhhh….*

Geoff says, "There has to be a way out of this. We don't have to hurt her."

Boyd shakes his head. "I've been thinking about doing this for a long time. She's the reason I ended up this way."

"That's not true," she says and buries her face in her hands. "I *love* you, son."

"Everyone needs to let go of things," Boyd says. "I've been letting go of things for a long time. I let go of Dad, I let go of my freedom, I let go of Odessa, and now I'm letting go of *you*."

"Odessa?"

"His girlfriend," Geoff says and points to Odessa's body which, in the darkness, resembles something like a heap of laundry.

"Oh my God. Oh my *God*."

Geoff tosses his shovel aside, out of anyone's reach. He faces Mrs. Renfro, raises his hands in what he hopes is a friendly gesture, and tells her, "I'm not going to hurt you. But you need to stay calm and keep your mouth shut. You're only making this worse."

Boyd, surprise in his voice, says, "I thought you had my back, man."

Geoff turns to him and offers the best friendly smile he can muster. "I'll always have your back. This isn't about me not having your back. But look at her. Look at your mom. She's a *person*, Boyd."

Boyd purses his lips and looks at her. Geoff can see the working gears in his head reflected in his face. But then he says, "A person? A *person*? Not to me."

"She has air in her lungs and blood in her veins. She has a heart and she *feels* things, and a brain where she thinks about you, I'm sure. She's all full of feelings, Boyd, and if you think about that, isn't it just amazing what makes up a person?"

Boyd just stares at her with an empty expression on his face.

Geoff says, "Remember when we were kids and she taught us how to fish with nothing but a piece of yarn and a wad of chewed up gum? There were no fish in the pond, but wasn't that fun anyways? And then that weekend she took us to the lake to fish off the dock and we caught something like fifty bluegills?"

Boyd lazily shifts his eyes to Geoff. "So? What's your point?"

"Well, I guess I mean that things weren't always so bad for you. You guys used to have fun together. So I know that somewhere inside you, you still feel something for her besides this rage."

Boyd says, "But…she'll call the cops."

"No — " Mrs. Renfro begins, but Geoff raises a hand to shush her.

"Maybe she will," Geoff says. "Maybe not. Maybe she loves you enough not to. I'd be willing to bet she just wants you to get help."

Boyd shakes his head. "Nope. No way. I already have a record. If I get arrested again, it's all over for me. There's no way to help me except to let me do this."

Geoff thinks about the years he's spent building his life, the lumps he took as a new employee at Gary's before making his way up the totem pole. He remembers getting offered the management position, how he couldn't stop grinning like a teenager getting lucky on prom night. He remembers that feeling of vindication, the confirmation that he'd made the right choice and that all the hard, long hours he'd put in lifting and maneuvering Williams-Sonoma sofas and La-Z-Boy recliners were really worth it because now he was somebody. And then the house in St. Ignace, how when he'd walked in the front door he'd known it was his, just a cheap place a few miles from the bridge, two stories on top of a crawlspace, a thousand square feet total, but damn it was worth it. It was all worth it because this was his life, this was who he was, all he had ever asked for, and people out there wish for a million dollars or to be President, but Geoff just wanted this quiet little life, had prayed for it, worked for it, and it was his, and it was a dream come true. Can he really let go of it now, just like that? Can he really turn his back on his dream in order to save his buddy, a guy he loves, sure, but someone who will clearly never amount to anything?

Geoff's heart sinks, but he smiles anyways because he's already made his choice, and realizing you've made a tough decision can be so freeing. Geoff had made his decision the first time he'd let Boyd back into his life seven years ago.

"Okay, I get it," Geoff says, "but if she calls the police we'll just make a run for it. We'll take off together and just start a new life somewhere, somehow."

"Easier just to end the bitch."

"Yeah but if we do that — think about it — we'll eventually have to go on the run anyways. Your mom and girlfriend going missing wouldn't be some big coincidence, Boyd. And with your record — well, they'd easily suspect you. Finding the bodies on the property would

81

be pretty damning evidence. Right? See what I mean?"

Boyd shrugs and takes a deep breath. "I've always done what I want."

Geoff reaches out, palms up. "Hand me the shovel. Give it to me. It's okay. There's no reason to hurt her. I don't want to. Let's just leave her here. We can take off right now. We'll go wherever you want. Come on. What's the one place you've always thought of going? Vegas? Cabo? Fucking Zimbabwe? I don't care what it is, Boyd. Let's just *go*."

Boyd laughs a little. "Yeah, Zimbabwe it is."

Geoff laughs, too, and then says, "Give me the shovel, Boyd."

"Okay," Boyd says and, with both hands, offers the shovel to Geoff. Geoff takes hold, but then Boyd gives it a small yank, holding tightly for a moment longer. Geoff looks into Boyd's eyes, eyes that, even in this darkness, appear to twinkle happily, though they also seem sinister and pathetically lost. Then Boyd says, "But I'm driving," and winks. He lets go of the shovel and Geoff tosses it aside, near the other one, which is well out of both Boyd's and Mrs. Renfro's reach.

"I won't call anyone," Mrs. Renfro says. "I won't."

Geoff says, "Come on, get up. Get out of here."

Mrs. Renfro, wasting no time, pushes through the trees, avoiding Boyd's general vicinity. Geoff watches her disappear through the thicket, out into the clearing again before reaching into his jeans pocket and withdrawing the car keys. He dangles them in front of Boyd and smiles as his friend snatches them.

"What about Odessa?" Geoff asks.

"We can put her in the trunk, find another place to bury her. There'll be a lot of forest and open road where we're going."

"Where's that? You weren't serious about Zimbabwe…?"

Boyd smiles. "I was thinking Idaho or Wyoming. Someplace like that. Somewhere where there aren't a whole lot of people around. Figured you'd like that."

Geoff smiles. "That's pretty much what I had in mind, too." Then, for some unfathomable reason, Geoff leans over and vomits a chunky, milky white slop onto the forest floor. Boyd laughs uproariously and pats Geoff on the back.

"Take it easy," he says. "Catch your breath. We'll pick up a bottled water on the way."

Geoff's stomach feels hot and tight, and the thought of ingesting anything — even water — nearly causes him to begin retching again. He burps a couple times and touches the back of his hand to his mouth. In a few moments, when he can speak again, he says, "I'll be fine," but when he looks up Boyd is gone.

Geoff pulls himself to his feet, cradling his churning stomach. He looks around, but there is no sign of his friend. He peers towards Odessa's body, but Boyd isn't there, either, and just as Geoff begins to truly wonder where his buddy has gone, he hears it. It's as if someone has dropped a hardcover book onto a wooden floor, a loud crack, and for one curious moment Geoff tries to reason that maybe it was the sound of a car door slamming, that maybe he'd left the driver's side door open earlier and Boyd only just now closed it. But then he hears the crack again, and reality crashes against him like a giant boulder. Geoff nearly loses his balance.

"No," he says to himself, denying what he already knows to be true, and rushes forward, back towards the clearing.

By the time Geoff pushes his way out of the

pines, Boyd is leaning against the barn, gazing downward, the revolver dangling from his right hand. *The gun*, Geoff thinks. *Jesus, I forgot all about the gun.*

As Geoff slows to a walk and approaches Boyd, his friend looks up at him and shrugs.

"Sorry, bro," he says. "I'm so sorry for you."

"What did you do?" Geoff asks, but then he sees Mrs. Renfro lying still in the snow beside the Impala. A pool of blood, black in the moonlight, collects in the snow around her head like an evil halo.

"You've got a good heart, Geoff. I look up to you, you know."

"What did you…. *Why*?"

Boyd shrugs again. "You were born with that heart. As for me? I was born with a stinger. Like a bee? I know it will doom me, but I have to use it."

"But…you said you wouldn't…."

Boyd smiles. "I never said that. Did I? All I know is you were right. You called it. We'll be running either way. Right? We'd have to get the fuck outta dodge even if we didn't kill Mom. At least this way I…like…*feel* better. If that makes

85

sense to you."

Geoff shakes his head, disbelief surging in him, his heart sinking. *What have I done*? he wonders. *Who is this person I let into my world*?

Boyd moves away from the barn and tosses Geoff a phone. Odessa's cellphone, all pink and glammed out with fake press-on diamonds. Even without bringing it to his nose he can smell her on it, the lovely aroma of her perfume. It's the odor of a person, a real person, who will never take another breath. Ever.

"Call Dallas," Boyd says. "Tell her we need a ride."

"A ride? What?"

"It's like this, man. You call Dallas, and I'll put these bitches in the trunk. Got me? You're with me, right?"

Geoff, confused, shakes his head. "I don't understand."

Boyd jabs a thumb to his right and says, "Mom and the gee-eff are going for a little swim in the pond."

Geoff looks at the pond, which is frozen over, and wonders if the ice can support the weight of the car. Then it occurs to him that,

86

well, it doesn't really matter. *Does anything matter anymore?*

"If it's gonna be a new life," Boyd says, "we'll have to get rid of your car. And Dallas. And then Dallas's car." He smiles, big bright white teeth, then walks nonchalantly towards the woods, presumably to retrieve Odessa's body.

For a moment Geoff wonders if Boyd will need help lifting the bodies and almost calls out, but then he halts himself, the sound of his shout catching in his throat like a cork. He sighs, leans his back against the barn, and slides down into a seated position atop the cold snow. He watches Boyd disappear into the darkness like some wandering demonic spirit.

Geoff opens Odessa's contacts, scrolls to Dallas, and stares at her name, wondering if he should — or even if he can — press the call button. After a minute or so, he glances over at Mrs. Renfro's body and realizes with some wonder that, even in the dim moonlight, her diamond ring is sparkling like a tiny lighthouse as if to signal to the lost that *hope is here, look to the horizon, set your course for the long, lonely journey ahead, everything's going to be all right.*

Geoff thinks, *She still wears it — after*

all these years, she still wears it, and then an unexpected moist heat rises in his face, pulling downward at the muscles in his cheeks. He has to close his eyes and slap himself to suppress a sob.

Geoff looks through watery eyes back towards the road, at the tire tracks which are, in the late-night darkness, quite faint. But they're there, oh yes, they are there, and Geoff wants very badly to attribute some kind of symbolic meaning to them, but the only thing he can muster now is a profound sadness, a sort of blank feeling through his core, like some weird blind spot, and — well — nothing makes sense.

He closes Odessa's contacts, opens the keypad, and tries to convince himself to dial nine-one-one. His thumb hovers over the 9 for a moment, but then, somehow, as if of its own volition, keys in his parents' home number.

A female voice answers on the third ring, and Geoff, struggling to keep his voice from breaking, says, "Mom? Mom, is that you?"

Campfire in Africa

)────────────(

I was in Africa, Gabon, to be exact. The moon was a silver sun. Guy was stuffing some sort of meat into his mouth, and in between bites he said, "Ibogaine, man. That's what we gave you." He said this in response to a comment I'd made about my head feeling smoky inside.

Guy's face was a red gleam in the firelight. His eyes were black. And there was something familiar about him.

I swatted at the air and said, "Jesus, these bugs."

Rhea, who looked familiar in her own way, laughed for some reason. So did Guy, which triggered an eruption from the Babongo. The Babongo, of course, couldn't understand a word we said, but laughter is a universal language.

"I don't see what's so funny," I said, but the six of them went on roaring. This must've lasted a minute or so. I've found that it's difficult to tell time when people are having fun at your expense.

Finally Rhea let out an exasperated gasp, a fake last-second laugh trailing off. She said, "Lighten up, Horse." Everyone calls me Horse because I lift weights and I wear my hair in a ponytail.

Guy was picking meat off a thin bone, baring his front teeth in an almost evil snarl. The Babongo watched us, the dark skin of their shoulders glimmering in the firelight. Sweat.

I pointed at one of them and said to Guy, "I don't feel bad for them. They're nearly naked. Look at my shirt." I lifted my arms so everyone could see the dark fabric where my fluids seeped through.

"The heat's a bear," Guy said. Rhea nodded.

The leader of the Babongo, a short fat man with thin, graying hair, poked at the fire with a long stick. A flock of orange sparks danced into the air. Hot wood made popping noises.

"So," I said, "this Ibogaine shit…"

Rhea said, "It comes from the root bark of

a plant. It's very common here, part of their culture."

"And you gave me some. In my water." I wasn't really asking. I was processing.

"In your water," Rhea confirmed.

One of the younger Babongo was staring at me. He was gaunt, but had a look about him that made me somewhat afraid. I think it was his confidence.

I grinned at him, hoping for the upper hand, and said, "Eyeing me down like I'm some kind of prey. Keep on eyeing me down, you bastard."

"They can't understand you." It was Guy. His voice suddenly seemed hollow.

"I know that."

Rhea was smiling and pulling this bowl thing to her lips, sipping. I noticed age lines around her lips, and I was reminded of a skull. A grinning skull.

"Tell me your age," I said to her, but she just let out a giggle. The Babongo started grinning, too — even the fucker who was staring at me in the same almost disinterested way civilized people would stare at a bowl of cereal.

91

I looked to Guy for support, but the fire was sweltering, an orange circle on his forehead. He looked a lot like Hunter S. Thompson without glasses on, and if Thompson had a whiskery beard.

Guy said, "We're in our fifties. But we can handle the terrain."

I nodded and glanced at the red coals at the base of the fire. "You're good guides. You'll get me where I'm going."

I was walking west to east across Africa. Gabon was my first stop. It was a sort of political thing. I was supposed to raise awareness for hunger in Africa. I was a disgraced Olympic runner (I'd won two individual silvers in 1992 and one bronze in 1996 in a team relay event) who'd been caught doping on stanozolol, the same steroid my contemporary, Ben Johnson, was caught using in 1988. And like Johnson, I was subsequently stripped of my medals. The most painful part of the whole thing wasn't the public disgrace, which sucked immensely — it was watching my 1996 teammates stripped of their bronze medals, especially my good buddy Gio, who actually broke down into a blubbering mess. Gio and I lost touch (I heard he actually fell into drugs himself after that, and in 2002, his parents, whom I never met, found him dead in his bedroom, asphyxiated on his own vomit), and I was so fucked up about everything that I became an advocate and snitch for the anti-doping community (sorry, Lance Armstrong).

I'd come to Africa for more reasons than just raising awareness for hunger. The main reason was probably that I thought the trip would improve my image, make people cheer for me again. The only problem was, according to my liaison officer — some uppity nigger named Ahman — that some religious tribe in Africa didn't want me there, some group Ahman called "The Forest People." And while knowing this definitely made me nervous, Ahman assured me that the indigenous people — even the most radical of them — lived by a code of peace.

"Because of the way American media portrays life in Africa, these Forest People may object to your being there," Ahman had said in his best I'm-better-than-you-voice, and I had to wonder how in the hell a guy like him could find such a cool, obviously good-paying job.

"Do I need a gun or something?" I'd asked.

"No. They'll never resort to violence. It's simply not their way."

"How exactly does the media portray

them?"

"As wild, uneducated, uncivilized savages," he'd said, and then smiled at me, a pearly white crescent in the middle of a face so black it gleamed purple when he perspired.

As it turned out, Guy and Rhea were from New York, but now lived in Africa. It seemed odd to see white faces. The news crews hadn't yet come, since my journey had just begun. A shitload of boats and other white people were waiting for me on the east coast, at the southern end of Somalia.

"We made eleven miles today," Guy said. He smirked at me. "You ever run eleven miles? What is that, about twenty-thousand meters? What was your best time? I mean, when you *weren't* doping."

I ignored his comment and looked away. The fat Babongo was jabbering away with the mean-looking one. My eyes felt thick.

"You understand them," I said to Guy, who nodded, chomping away at a new piece of meat — something that resembled a very small chicken leg, something I imagined to be roughly the size of Andre the Giant's thumb. "Tell me what they're saying."

"They like your hair," he said.

I touched my ponytail, waved it around like a lasso. The Babongo laughed like children. "They aren't very smart, are they?" I said. "And look how fat that one is. I thought Africans were going hungry. That's what all the commercials tell you. You know, little children with flies circling their faces, flecks of rice in the corners of their mouths."

"They're leaving soon," Rhea said.

I had a canteen of water next to me, but when I reached for it, it felt like my arm just kept going on and on. Eventually I was able to snatch it up, and I gulped, knowing full well there was this Ibogaine shit in it.

"You're gonna get in trouble," I told them. "You can't drug people's canteens. You're sabotaging my quest."

"It's just to help you relax and get some rest for tomorrow," Rhea said. "You'll sleep easier."

I leaned back. The moon was as round as a cookie. It seemed just out my reach, no further away than the canteen had been.

"I'm tired of listening to them and their gibberish," I said, referring to the Babongo.

"It's Tsogo," Guy said. "They're speaking Tsogo."

"What-the-fuck-ever," I said, putting my hands behind my head. The stars looked like they were floating in rough seas. There were waves and everything.

"You finished your meat?" Guy asked.

"I did," I said. "It was fine. What is it anyway?"

Guy smirked and stared at me for a few seconds. "It's human," he said finally, and we all burst into hysterical laughter.

When I regained control of myself, I pointed at the Babongo. "What about them?" I asked. "I haven't seen them eating."

Rhea said, "This tribe is vegetarian. The only meat they eat is fish."

I glared at the Babongo. The four of them were getting mixed up in some sort of conversation now. One of them seemed to be telling a story. The other three listened intently.

"How long have you guys been out here?" I asked my guides. "How long have you lived in Africa?"

Guy and Rhea looked at each other for a moment, and both of them smirked and looked down into the fire. Rhea sipped from her bowl-thing again.

"We came out about twelve years ago," Guy said finally. "Just dropped everything and left our old life behind in New York."

"Wow," I said. "Just wow."

Rhea said, "Our son died, and we just had to get away from there, so we came here to try and understand what life is all about. We figured if we gave up all our technologies and comforts, maybe we'd figure out not only why our son had to die, but why he'd lived, too."

"I'm sorry to hear that," I said, and it felt like I really was. I think I wanted to be, but I couldn't possibly fathom that kind of catastrophe. I couldn't quite comprehend her hippie-talk, either, all this nonsense about the meaning of life and living out in the elements.

"We know the land," Guy said. "When we heard you were coming here, a big celebrity like yourself…well, we just had to volunteer as your guides."

This comment flattered me, because I really wasn't much of a celebrity. It was 2014, long after the whole doping debacle. And those who did remember me generally held me in contempt for cheating.

"I'm just trying to overcome my past," I told them, fighting a sudden inexplicable wave of exhaustion. "I made some mistakes, and I'm here to, I don't know, make myself look good again."

Rhea laughed a little and Guy smiled. I looked over at the Babongo and saw that one of them was gnawing at some kind of thick leaf. While the leaf definitely didn't look appetizing, I felt a stirring in my stomach and became jealous. And anyways, I figured, another meal might revitalize me, lift me out of the sudden sleepy haze that had overwhelmed me.

"I'm still hungry," I said to Rhea. "Make me a hamburger or something."

There was an exaggerated eruption of laughter again, but before I could join in I drifted off into a blankness I can't even describe.

I snapped awake and for a moment. I was full of intense fear and confusion. The sun beat down. A hot wind slipped by my face like bad breath.

My head felt heavy, my neck weak. I tried

raising myself up, struggling to control the movement of my head, but it was a futile effort. Sleep still clung to the sides of my vision. I had the notion that I was feeling some after effects of the drug. I began to worry that I had overdosed, but within minutes I began to feel better.

I lifted my head and glanced around. Everything was still and silent. I wondered about wildlife, if I was too exposed, if perhaps I'd be something's next meal.

The fire was still going, but it was much smaller. There was something cooking over it, a half-eaten extension of meat held up by fork-tipped props that had been stuck in the ground.

Guy, Rhea, and the Babongo were gone. It felt as if they'd never existed, what with how still and quiet it was.

"Hey," I called, but I was too nervous to raise my voice on the off chance a pride of lions were hanging around somewhere close dreaming of a meal that wasn't antelope, or whatever the hell those deer things are.

I noticed a piece of paper on my chest, held in place by my canteen. The paper's corners fluttered in the wind. I lifted it, unfolded it.

It said, "Somalia's a hop, skip, and a jump from here. How fast can you get there now?" Guy had printed his name at the bottom.

I didn't understand. I crumpled the paper up and tossed it towards the fire, but the wind made it curve away. It rolled away into the long grass.

I sat up, with some effort, because I couldn't move my left leg. Then it occurred to me…

Initially there was no real fear or terror, just the sensation of an unexpected discovery. It was like when you hear a celebrity dies young. You care, but not really. That's what it was like for those first two seconds before I realized what was going on.

A white bandage around a round stump. Pinkish fluid seeping through. And the remains of my leg baking over a campfire.

Spiral

)————————(

Pike was picking paint chips off the doorframe and sticking them in his mouth. He was slouched over against the wall and higher than I'd ever seen him, which was saying something. This was one of those times I seriously considered calling an ambulance, like those two times with Olek over a year-and-a-half ago. With Olek I had waited too long both times, and he barely survived both times. Ever since then I've lived by two rules: One, I will never, ever get that high; and two, it's better to call nine-one-one *before* the OD happens. I guess you could call those rules.

Olek was sitting next to me with this sullen look on his face and he was staring at Pike. Olek said, "Hey, bro, you know I'm here for you," but Pike didn't look up and in all honesty probably didn't even hear him. Then it occurred to me that maybe Olek was talking to me, but I didn't respond to him either.

Olek had gone straight-edge. Funny that it took two hospital stays for him to clean up, but whatever. I know as well as anyone how hard it is to kick habits. Fool me once, fool me twice, and all that. I hadn't even been fooled once yet, if OD-ing means getting fooled.

The thing about Olek this time was I wasn't sure why he was here. He just kind of came over of his own accord, and I let him in because that's what you do for old friends. But with him being clean now the atmosphere felt wrong, like a running aquarium with no fish in it.

"He's out of it," I said to Olek, and he kind of grinned then, but he still looked sad and older than I remembered him.

Olek used to have bleach-blond hair cut down to about a quarter-inch or so. Real short. Now it was brown, and he wore it long, just above his shoulders, and it looked really clean, like those girls you see in shampoo commercials. He was all dressed up in this gray suit, too, looking very 1980s Don Johnson, and I couldn't help but wonder if he'd scrapped all his old Def Leppard and Metallica t-shirts, if this *Miami Vice* look was normal for him now. He looked very different from how he used to, sure,

102

but he still had those bags under his eyes. He wore those things like scars.

Pike's right arm went up, and he scratched at the doorframe with his thumbnail before sticking it into his mouth. He looked like he was biting his nails, but what he was really doing was scraping the paint off onto his teeth.

"Think we should call someone?" I asked, lifting a joint to my lips. Bluish plumes of smoke surrounded my head like clouds.

"No," Olek said. I noticed that he'd put on weight. I hadn't seen the guy in a few months.

"I've never seen him like this. I haven't seen it so bad since…well, since last year when it was you. Ya know?"

Olek laughed, but it sounded more like a sniff, like he had a runny nose. He said, "He'll be fine. Everything'll be fine."

Just then there was a knock at the door, which startled Pike a little, and he wavered for a second before he fell backwards and kind of rolled from his ass to his back. I laughed a little, but Olek didn't make a sound.

"It's open," I said without getting up from the sofa, and the door opened somewhat slowly, as if someone was afraid to come in.

Pike lifted his right arm up and draped it over his face, covering his eyes. I could see the track marks going down the side of his pale white wrist, which I believe is where the cephalic vein is. I learned about all that anatomical stuff later. Pike's chest was heaving up and down. Pike was very muscular back then and the position he was lying in made it look like he had tits.

Ambrosia walked in and Olek stood up to greet her. She was an abnormally tall black woman, well over six feet, but she was quite thin and attractive. She was wearing a black skirt and a red blouse, very professional looking, as if she'd just come here from work, but I had forgotten what her job was. Lawyer or secretary or something like that. I always thought she had nice eyes, how you could see the whole iris floating atop the whiteness like little brown islands. I couldn't help but wonder, as I did often, why she was all caught up with a short, stocky white guy, especially one like Pike who had this kind of problem.

When she walked in, she had this disbelieving scowl on her face, and she was looking at Pike who was, of course, whacked out on the floor.

Olek said, "I'm glad you made it."

"You invited her?" I said. I wasn't that happy to see her, not when her husband was so high he couldn't function. I was embarrassed for him.

"When did you invite her?" I asked, but then I remembered how Olek was texting after he got here.

Ambrosia said, "What did it this time?"

Olek looked at me and raised his eyebrows. He'd only gotten here after Pike was already done shooting up, so this was Olek's way of asking me the same question Ambrosia just asked, though he surely knew what Pike was on. Coy motherfucker.

I said, "Heroin. It was a whole lot of heroin."

There was a moment of silence then in which I could hear Pike's breathing, how it seemed like he was laboring a little, but it might've been that peculiar position he was lying in on the wood-planked floor restricting his airway. That moment of silence was kind of nice, though. It was one of those times when you can just take everything in, and it makes you realize you just might find something in your life to expel everything that infects you.

"Think we should call nine-one-one?" I asked again since Ambrosia was here now and it was more her responsibility to say so than it was Olek's.

She shook her Jheri-curled head and said, "No, I've seen it before. Just get me a glass of water."

I stood up and went to the kitchen, which was pretty much just an extension of my apartment's living room, and filled a foggy glass with tap water. When I came back out I extended it to Ambrosia and said, "How long till he's okay?" I was as much an addict as Pike or Olek ever were, but I never used heroin before, and I knew Ambrosia had seen her husband close to like this at least a few times.

"He's already asleep, so I'd say four, five, maybe six hours." She took the glass of water from me and poured the fluid onto Pike's head.

He jerked and spluttered for a moment, his hazel eyes wide, then muttered something about us being open-chested cowards, whatever that meant. He was staring at Ambrosia, and the way he looked it was like he thought everything was an eruption of dreams, like some volcano in his head finally blew, and I knew this was trouble because once a volcano's top comes off there's no repairing it.

Ambrosia knelt down next to him and said, "Pete," because "Pike" was short for Pete Iker.

"Hey, Pete," she said and squeezed his cheeks with fingers that had white-painted nails as pointy as shark's teeth. "Hey, look at me. It's me. Time to get up. It's time to go home now."

But Pike didn't get up or anything. He just rolled onto his side into the fetal position and started going back to sleep. He looked like an enormous baby, and I thought *Let's get him his blankie*.

Ambrosia hooked her hand around his shoulder and tried to yank him back over, but he was too powerful for her. She kept saying, "Pete, come on, Pete. Peter Iker, look at me," and stuff like that, things you might say to get a little kid's attention. It was all very embarrassing. I knew Pike would be all humiliated and angry about it once he came to. Pike always had this attitude about him, like some meathead, and I always thought that's what big muscles do to you.

Olek knelt down by them, and I joined them right after I finished smoking. I laid the remaining unsmokable part of the roach on the coffee table and moved over by Olek, who had an arm around Ambrosia's shoulder. He was rubbing his hand up and down on her arm, and it occurred to me that he was consoling her, and they were muttering about carrying Pike out of there.

"Help us," Olek said, and so I did.

*

Two days later my manager, Waldo, stopped me from bagging groceries and said I had a phone call. He plucked a customer's can of peas from my hand and said, "Go ahead, I got this." Then he started stuffing the lady's groceries into bags with a speed and intensity that told me I would never amount to anything.

It was Olek on the phone fulfilling his promise to me: "Just wanted to keep you updated," he told me. "It was an OD, and they said we were lucky we got him to the hospital when we did."

"I told you we should call someone," I said.

"No, to be fair, you asked if we should."

"And you both said not to."

Olek sighed. "I don't want to debate. But anyways, Pike's being discharged tomorrow morning. He's been up and around today and seems pretty much fine."

"He left his drugs at my apartment."

Olek carried on as if he hadn't heard me. "He's being admitted at Montego tomorrow. It's time to get him right."

Montego was the local rehab facility, a pretty legit place from what I'd heard. That's where Olek had ended up, and now he was working there, according to the conversation I'd had with him right before he and Ambrosia had driven away from my apartment the other day, Pike looking like a dead fish on the back seat of Olek's Buick. *I got a job there*, Olek had told me. *Define irony*, I'd replied.

"I get out soon," I said. "I'll come down to the hospital in a couple hours, see what's what."

Olek sighed again. "Yeah, well sure, but I'm not sure that's a good idea right now."

"What's the matter?"

"I just mean, well, we're trying to clean him up, so it's probably not best for him to be around you right now. I'm not trying to be mean or anything."

Waldo's office was cluttered and quite disgusting, with the cracked brick walls and no

109

windows and the documents and completed job applications strewn about the desk. His ancient computer's screensaver painted colorful shapes against a black background. I smelled cigarettes.

"Maybe," I said, and laughed a little because I was feeling nervous and not sure I was the commitment type. "Maybe I could get clean, too."

Olek sighed for the third time, like a parent who is frustrated with his toddler. "For sure, man, I don't want to discourage you, but this is all about Pike right now. Let's just worry about him. Okay? Then we'll start talking about you. I'd like that."

I thought about Pike's heroin stash, which he'd left sitting on the floor in my bathroom. There were a couple needles, a fat greenish colored rubber band, a blackened spoon, a lighter that looked like a miniature blowtorch, and two pouches of powder which was the drug itself. All of this was in a little wooden box that looked like a jewelry box and it had an engraving on top of it that read, "To my muscle-man" and beneath that, "- AI," which were Ambrosia's initials.

"What can I do to prove myself to you?" I asked.

110

Olek laughed then, which was a nice sound that relieved me a little. It was a friendly laugh. Then he said, "It's not about proving anything. We'll get you squared away. Don't worry about it, brother."

After we hung up, I stood there rubbing my sweaty palms on my green apron. I was staring at Waldo's screensaver, and I kept thinking about Pike's box, wondering what in the world he would use it for now.

*

About a month later I called Montego to check on Pike. I hadn't heard from Olek or Ambrosia since the phone call at work, so I was quite concerned and curious about why no one had contacted me. I would've driven down to see him, but Montego's website said they didn't allow visitors during the detox period, which could last up to a month, but I figured what the hell, it's been a month, so it should be safe to call.

The lady on the phone, who introduced herself as Frieda, asked for some information, so I told her I was Pike's older brother, Kory, who we sometimes jokingly called "Kike." Kory and Pike weren't very close, but I had a hunch he'd be on Pike's approved list of contacts, and I was right. I got Kory's date of birth off Facebook and recited it to the Frieda lady, and it was simple as that.

When Pike answered he sounded different, kind of excited, like maybe it was really his brother on the phone and he appreciated the call. "Kory?" he said in that happy voice, but I told him it wasn't and to keep quiet about it.

"How are they treating you in there?" I asked.

He took a deep breath and said, "Pretty good. It's not that bad, really." But something in his voice had changed, and I could tell he was probably fibbing.

"Listen, Pike, I've got your box still. I hid it in the bathroom ceiling."

"The ceiling?"

"Yeah, above a tile. I hid it in case someone comes by, the cops or something." I had figured Olek and Ambrosia had to give a statement or something when Pike was admitted to the hospital for OD-ing, but I hadn't yet heard from any police about it.

"That's good," Pike said. "Keep it out of sight."

"Not a problem. I haven't touched it or anything, either. I'm saving it for when you get out, if you still want it."

"Yeah, about that," he said, and then he hesitated. There was a shuffling noise like he was shifting the telephone from one ear to the other. "I probably won't need it, man. You keep it."

"I can't do that. I guess I can pay you for it, though." I wasn't against trying heroin. *Might actually be nice in moderation*, I thought.

Pike laughed, but he sounded pretty tired and humorless. "No, no, I don't want your money."

There was a pause then, and I was trying to think of what to say, but all I could think of was, "How much longer till you're out?"

"Another couple months," he said. "Fifty-eight more days. The people here are great. They really know what they're doing."

"How are the treatments or whatever?"

"Fine, it's just like, you get together with counselors and other fuck-ups and talk about stuff. That's the best part because I get to realize my life isn't nearly as bad as some of these other sad-sacks."

I laughed. It was good to hear the old Pike again, that annoyed twinge in his voice. "You were pretty whacked out that day, though."

"Yeah, well."

There was another weird pause then, and I could tell Pike was trying to say something. I could picture him standing there with his mouth open, trying to spit out whatever it was he wanted to talk about. I waited while the empty static of the open phone line crackled in my ear.

Finally, Pike said, "They want me to go by 'Pete' now. They said Pike is from my old life. But you can call me whatever you want."

I smiled at that because it meant we were brothers, but I still had to ask, "Hey, when you get out, will we still be, ya know, the same?"

"In some ways, yeah, I want to. We can still hang a couple times a week, like always. But... well...whatever they're doing here, it's kind of working. For the first time in forever it feels like my head's clear, like, I don't know — like there were mosquitos in my head and these people helped them get out of there."

"Weird," I said.

He laughed. "Yeah, very. But...do you have any idea what drugs do to you? Like, to your brain and your body? They said shooting up can leave silver lines up and down your arms from when you miss the vein. Stuff like that. They said that's probably why my skin was so pale…."

Pike kind of lost me then, going on and on about anatomical stuff, but the last thing I caught was something about the cephalic vein on his wrist. I drifted away from him and felt an urge to dig out my Vicodin. The bottle was in my bedroom, in my nightstand's drawer. I'd bought them off some guy named Arthur a while back, maybe six months ago, but only used a couple of them in that time. I was more the weed and coke type, but popping pills and shooting up weren't my thing.

I was staring at the entrance to my bedroom, at the soft light coming in through the window like some divine spotlight beckoning me to go in there, when I noticed Pike was done talking. I said, "Wow, that's amazing," not really knowing what was amazing at all.

"Yeah. Hey, listen. I need you to swing by my place and check on Am for me. She's been acting funny. If you could just go by there a couple times and like spy on her, see what she's up to. Don't tell her I sent you. Don't even let her know you're there."

"Acting funny?"

"Yeah, when she comes to visit. I can't really explain it, but something's off. She's like, I don't know, distant. Like she might be mad at me for all this. I tried to kiss her a couple days ago, and she turned away a little so I only got the corner of her mouth."

Pike and Ambrosia had been going through some sort of tribulation before his OD. He'd been talking about it for a few weeks, maybe a month. He'd said it was about all the time he was spending at my place, and the fact that she'd found the spare key I'd given him in case he ever needed to come by when I wasn't home. He'd encouraged me not to worry about it, that she was just the needy and clingy type. He'd said it wasn't a huge deal since we only hung out a couple times a week anyways. He'd said she'd get over it, but judging by this conversation she was still giving him more issues, as if he shouldn't be completely focused on his time at Montego.

"Jesus, Pike, when does it end? Sure, sure, I'll go by there."

He thanked me, and that was pretty much the end of our conversation, since after that he told me his time was up, and I said, "Christ,

116

what is it, prison?" But then he just laughed and said goodbye, and I said I'd call him after I looked in on Ambrosia.

After that I popped two Vicodin and stretched out on my bed. I put the TV on the Tigers game, but in a few minutes I was too out of it for baseball. I just remember spinning in time with the earth after that, and this glorious little tickle in my belly.

*

So a couple days later, on Saturday night, I drove out to the Ikers' house, which was this small white house out in the country, away from the city. It was about a twenty minute drive from my apartment in the city. The place was quite tiny, which was part of the reason I never visited there much, what with the way cramped spaces make me feel, but the real reason was that Pike and I could never hang out and get high with Ambrosia around. It was for that reason that I tried to plant this little seed in Pike's head for a few years that the bitch wasn't any good for him, but I never came right out and said he should divorce her or anything. But since they'd been fighting and having issues in their marriage, I couldn't help but feel somewhat happy about it, and maybe even a little sense of pride, too, because it was probably my doing in some way. It was kinda like in the movies, how sometimes it's not just the good guy against the bad guy. Sometimes there's a third party that represents a grayer area somewhere between good and bad, and that third party will come in and turn the good guy against the bad guy, and the good guy and bad guy will have this battle and hurt each other real bad, and then the third party is the one left standing. The third party gets to rule the universe. I was feeling kinda like that third party.

I parked my Ranger at the curb across the street, one house over. My truck wasn't necessarily the most recognizable vehicle around, and I wasn't even sure if Ambrosia had ever seen it before, but I didn't want to risk it. Parking one house down, I figured, made it less likely she'd notice. She probably couldn't see me through the driver's side window in the darkness, and she'd probably think I was just visiting a neighbor.

Being a bit further down the road, of course, made it harder for me to see into the front window, and anyways I didn't know what exactly I was looking for. Pike had just asked me to keep an eye on Ambrosia and see what she was up to, which sounded interesting but would probably be more boring than sitting around in my apartment smoking weed, which was objectionably boring when I was alone, especially when there wasn't a ballgame on. If I could see anything at all — and I couldn't, yet — it would probably just be Pike's wife slouched back on the couch eating ice cream watching *L.A. Law* reruns on A&E. And as much as I could appreciate the genius of Corbin Bernsen, this did not sound like a fun Saturday night out on the town.

After over an hour of sitting in uncomfortable silence, looking around from time to time because I felt paranoid and exposed, nothing had yet happened, and I began to lament the idea of spending any more time sitting there. I wanted to leave, but Pike was my friend, and I'd always been loyal to my best friends, and there was no reason to punk out yet, and anyways I was really hoping I'd dig up some dirt on Ambrosia, something good that would ruin their marriage. Then it would be just me and my chum. Fuck Olek, he was a quitter. I still liked Olek, but I had lost a lot of respect for him, too. When things get scary and hard we should see them through, because when you give up and move on from something you're really just lying to yourself, restricting who you truly are deep down in your heart. That's what I learned from that show *Criminal Minds*. Killers can't help themselves, can't stop killing, because that's who they, are and that's what they really want. Everyone has that one thing. Doing drugs was ours, and at least Pike and I were happy — maybe not Pike anymore, I guessed, since he was in rehab, God bless his soul — but Olek was lying to himself and because of that he'd never live another happy day in his life. Much better to descend into drug-addled madness, spinning down into that vibrant abyss one last time. Kiss the sun and the skyline goodbye, you're taking a trip into heaven's spiral, and there you'll live forever and ever, life without end, cross your heart hope to fly.

Just as I cracked the driver's side window and resigned myself to smoke a joint, Olek's giant Buick came rolling up. The damn thing was unmistakable, just this huge cream-colored yacht-on-wheels. Instead of reaching into my shirt pocket, I slouched down and watched the vehicle hang a left into Ambrosia's driveway. The brake lights brightened into twin planets, dimmed back to normal, then shut off completely as Olek killed the engine. When he got out I noticed he was carrying a brown paper bag, the big kind you get at the grocery store. It didn't seem too heavy, but he was cradling it under one arm as if he was afraid the bottom would fall out. He took it to the doorstep, either knocked or rang the doorbell, I couldn't tell,

120

and before long the porch light came on and Ambrosia opened the door.

Olek leaned in and kissed her cheek, and for the next minute or so they appeared to be discussing something, but then Ambrosia stepped out of the way and let Olek in. I craned my neck around hoping to see into the front window better, but Ambrosia walked over and closed the curtains.

"That's weird," I said to myself, and it really was. I mean, why would they need privacy?

I hung around for a while longer, maybe a half hour, before I began to wonder if Olek would ever leave. Then I remembered the way Olek was consoling Ambrosia back at my place, back when Pike had his little episode. My mind kept flashing an image of Olek's hand moving up and down Ambrosia's arm, and suddenly my heart felt like hot wax.

"You motherfuckers," I said, trying to control my breathing. Poor Pike. Poor, poor Pike. They came and took away everything that had ever defined him, tossed him into a rehab facility, and now they were fucking each other, enjoying their little vacation away from my best buddy. And now I'd have to be the one to tell him.

121

It took me a good five minutes to convince myself not to go tear the front door down. The deciding factor was the fact that, yes, I was upset for my friend because I knew the news would hurt him, but I was also happy to uncover some incriminating evidence against Ambrosia, the kind of thing that would most certainly destroy the marriage. So instead of confronting Olek and Ambrosia, I lit my roach, smoked about half of it, and drove home trying to think of a good way to break the news to Pike.

*

Considering the stress I was under, I slept pretty well that night. There was an initial period of time, maybe an hour, when I couldn't quite fall asleep. I kept trying to decide if I should call Pike right away, or wait until the next day. Aside from the fact that I was relatively excited to set the breakup ball in motion, this was the kind of information you shouldn't keep from someone in Pike's position. But at the same time, he was in a rehab facility, so it seemed inappropriate somehow to call so late. Pike probably had an assigned bedtime. And anyways, it wasn't a medical emergency and there hadn't been a death in the family or anything, so I eventually decided the call could wait until the following day. After that I fell asleep and didn't wake up for a good nine hours.

It was early Sunday afternoon, just past one, before I built up enough courage to place the call. The Frieda lady answered again and, like before, I told her I was Kory Iker. Within a couple of minutes Pike picked up.

I told him about going to his house and checking in on Ambrosia, and he asked how it went.

"I hope you're sitting down."

"What? Why?"

"Are you sitting down?"

Pike paused for a second and then said, "Yeah, man, I am. What's going on? Something wrong?"

"Well, I saw something. Are you sure you're sitting down? If I was you I'd want to be sitting down."

"Jesus, man, spit it out."

I sat back on my couch and looked up at the ceiling. "It's about your wife."

There was a pause again, and then Pike said, "Um, yeah, I already got that impression. What is it?"

Why was I being so hesitant? Was it because

123

part of me thought I should break the bad news to him in person? I knew I wouldn't like to find out over the phone that my wife was cheating on me. But, really, what did it matter? This wasn't the kind of news anyone would want to hear, no matter how you told them, whether it was over the phone, in person, or via singing telegram.

"Maybe I should drive out and tell you in person," I said.

"Jesus Christ, you're killing me here. Would you just tell me what the hell's going on already, before I hang up on your dumb ass?"

I took a breath. "Ambrosia. She's, uh…she's cheating on you." Pike didn't say anything. "Hey, Pike, you still there? Did you hear me?"

His voice went low. "I knew it. I fucking knew it."

"I know it's not easy. It can't be easy hearing this kind of thing."

"Who?" he asked. "Did you see him? What does he drive? I'll find him. I swear to God I'll find him."

I took another breath and laughed a little, nervously. "That's the thing," I said. "I mean… Pike, seriously, maybe you should just take some time to calm down. You need to think

124

about what you need to do next."

"I know what I'm doing next. I'm gonna hunt this guy down and beat him like no one's ever been beat before."

An image of Pike, with all his enormous muscles, pummeling the shit out of Olek passed through my mind. I could see the blood oozing out of Olek's nose and mouth, his eyes swelling shut as he pleaded with Pike to stop. As much as I couldn't blame the guy, however, I knew it would be a bad idea for this to come to a violent conclusion. It would be much better for everyone if Pike just cut ties with Ambrosia *and* Olek, let them do their thing, forget about them forever and come on back home to my place, where we could get back to our lives.

"Hey, Pike, I know you're pissed, but maybe the best thing to do here is just calm down and ask for a divorce."

Pike laughed sarcastically. "A *divorce*? You're kidding me, right?"

I laughed too. "No, no joke. I mean, if I found out my wife was banging some other dude, I'd be out."

"Wait, could you repeat yourself? I'm not sure you were quite insensitive enough there."

"Sorry. But really, why would you *want* to stick around? Look what she did with you, Pikey."

"What she did. What do you mean by that?"

I sat up and clicked on the television, then muted it. It was past game time. "She tossed you into rehab so she could start fucking around easier."

There was a moment of silence, as if we were mourning a death. On the television Justin Verlander threw a strike and froze the Minnesota Twins batter. The umpire called strike three, and the batter started arguing silently. I fought the urge to unmute the TV, but then the broadcast faded out and was replaced by a commercial for a paint product.

"You okay, Pike?" I asked. "Processing everything?"

He took a deep breath that sounded like a stiff ocean breeze. "I'm fine. I think. Maybe not. I just…I don't really know what to think. Are you sure you saw what you think you did? Could it be a mistake?"

I thought about Olek leaning in to plant a peck on Ambrosia's chocolatey cheek. "I doubt it," I said.

126

The Tigers game came back on, bottom of the third, Detroit already up three to zero. Miguel Cabrera was taking his warmup swings before his second at-bat. The statistical overlay revealed that he'd already hit a two-run homer.

"Seriously, though," Pike said, "who was it? Who's the guy? Someone we know?"

"I really shouldn't tell — "

Pike cut me off. "I need to know. I know you don't understand, but after all I've been through here… My life's falling apart. It's like I fell asleep in your apartment and woke up in this hell-hole, and now I'm supposed to be this different person. Know what I mean? Like, I have to let go of my past, and that's okay to a point — I know I need to wise up a little — but this is too much. You're talking about divorce, and I don't even know what the fuck is going on here. How can I let go of my wife right now?"

"You got me, you know."

Pike laughed, but this time I couldn't tell if it was sarcastic or genuine. "Just tell me who the guy is. I can tell you know who he is, which means I probably do, too. If you do that much for me, then at least I might be able to make a logical decision. Eventually."

Cabrera muscled a single into right field. I sighed, frustrated because I couldn't enjoy the game, not with Pike's uncharacteristic pleading. I wasn't liking the sober Pike at all.

"Come on," Pike said. "She's my wife, man. My *wife*. I know I don't talk about her a lot, but if you've ever been in love — *have* you ever been in love? — you'll understand why I need to know. And anyways, you know…I might want to have a family with her someday."

The truth was, yes, I *had* been in love once. At least I thought so. It was back in the eighth grade and her name was Cindy, and it was a forbidden love because she was my second-cousin. We kissed once in the park, and it was this incredible magical moment, like fairy dust and ice cream cones that don't melt. After our kiss, I lit a joint and offered her a hit, but she turned me down, and she was acting all shy all of a sudden. Then she made me promise not to tell anyone about our kiss, and she pretty much never talked to me again. There were times I'd try to catch up with her after school, but she was always busy with this anti-drug campaign thing, so she always gave me the cold shoulder. Eventually I just had to say fuck her, and I moved on. But I never loved anyone like that again.

The memory of Cindy filled me with a weird emotion that made me feel as if I were encased in mud, made my muscles all stiff and tired. Then, for whatever reason — maybe because I felt bad, or maybe because I finally felt like I could empathize with Pike — I blurted, "It was Olek."

I heard Pike gasp, the sound of the air stopping in his throat. "What if...? What if it's...if it's...*not mine...*?"

Pike hung up.

*

For lunch I ate a tuna fish sandwich, a bowlful of salt and vinegar potato chips, and a couple happy pills, washing everything down with a tall glass of cranberry juice. The game went on pretty much as expected, with Verlander dominating Minnesota through eight innings before some reliever I'd never heard of took over in the ninth. The Tigers won seven to one. Verlander struck out ten and only gave up three hits. Cabrera finished with four runs batted in.

And despite the game, which should have made me feel very happy and at ease with the universe, I couldn't shake this dreadful butterfly feeling in my stomach. I kept imagining Pike taking a baseball bat to Olek's longhaired head.

129

I was kicking myself for letting Olek's name slip. And while some part of me was certainly worried about Olek's physical well-being, I was more worried about Pike doing something that would lead to an arrest and time in prison. The whole point of telling him about the affair was so I could spend more time with him. That wasn't going to happen if Pike was locked up.

Fortunately, I figured, Pike was locked up in rehab, surrounded by positive thoughts and professionals who encouraged self-forgiveness and all that hogwash. He'd have plenty of time and opportunity to cool his head, and then in a few weeks, after he was released, we could get on with our drug-addled lives.

Later that evening, while working the closing shift at the store, Waldo relieved me from bagging groceries again because I had another phone call. Thinking it was probably Pike, I rushed to the manager's office and picked up the receiver.

"Hey, it's Olek. Listen, do you know where — "

"Eat me," I said before slamming the phone down and returning to work.

*

I spent the rest of my shift feeling quite satisfied with myself. Olek tried to call me back twice, but I told Waldo to tell him I'd left for the night. Waldo had asked me if everything was okay, suggesting that if there was an emergency I could go home, but I'd assured him that everything was fine and finished out my shift, which ended at midnight.

I pulled into the drive at my apartment complex just as Van Halen's "Right Now" came on the classic rock station, the epic piano intro filling me with the reassuring feeling that, yes, I *was* a badass for letting Olek have it earlier. I kept thinking that if I were a character in a movie, "Right Now" would be the song the director would use to introduce me. The slow-mo camera would pan up from my feet, and I'd be wearing this black suit and tie, and I'd have my hair slicked back, a gun pointed out in front of me, ready to wipe out a room full of gangsters.

As I walked up the stairs to my second-floor apartment, I imagined myself fighting my way to the evil mob boss, played by Olek. I imagined tying him up and beating him senseless, commanding him to tell me why he'd ruined Pike's life, and where he'd dumped Ambrosia's body. Olek would be tough in his own way, so he'd be unwilling to give up any information easily, which meant I'd have to torture it out of him. I imagined pulling his teeth out with pliers, slipping razorblades beneath his fingernails, and poking fishhooks through his eyelids. After that Olek would tell me everything, and I'd put a bullet in his traitorous brain.

When I arrived at my apartment door, I was shocked to find it was unlocked. For a few disorientating moments I was convinced that I'd been burglarized, but as I stepped over the threshold and saw that nothing seemed out of place, I resigned myself to the idea that I'd simply forgotten to lock up behind myself earlier. I flicked on an overhead light, but then I noticed the soft white light of the bathroom's fluorescent lightbulbs seeping into the living area from under the closed door. This was a problem because, for one, I never closed the bathroom door when I was home alone, and for two, I certainly wouldn't have left the light on, since it was still daytime when I'd left for work. The bathroom window always let in light, so I really never needed the bathroom lights unless it was dark outside.

I froze for a few moments, wondering if I should call out, see if anyone answered me. I eventually decided, probably irrationally, to check the door, see if it was unlocked, and as I crept towards the bathroom, I passed by my

132

couch and coffee table. I glanced at the coffee table and froze again, staring at the small metal object lying there. A key. The spare key I'd given Pike a long time ago.

"Pike?" I called, raising my voice a little. "Pike, you in there?"

When he didn't answer, I went to the door and checked the knob. It was unlocked, so I opened it slowly. "Pike?" I said again as I pushed the door open.

The first thing I saw was the gap in the ceiling where a tile had been, and then the tile itself cracked into two halves in the bathtub. As I pushed the door open further I saw Pike lying on the floor, a curious expression on his square-jawed face, his eyes fixed on a spot on the ceiling above him. The contents of Pike's heroin box were strewn about the room and one of the fat rubber bands was tied around his arm. The syringe was still sticking out of the crook of his elbow, right beneath the rubber band. The heroin box itself had been destroyed. Chunks and slivers of stained wood lay near the side of the ceramic bathtub, where, it appeared, Pike must have thrown the box, smashing it into as many pieces as he could.

"Jesus, Pike, why didn't you wait for me?"

I said as I walked into the room. Then I realized that he hadn't even responded to my presence yet, and a heavy feeling of dread fell over me.

"Pike?" I said again, but then I noticed his lips.

Pike's mouth was open, little flecks of something around his blue lips. It took a moment for it to register that he'd overdosed again, vomited, and choked. My friend was dead and had probably been so for a few hours, judging by the way his skin felt when I touched his cheek.

At first I could only stand over him, staring into his empty eyes, wondering if I could have done something to prevent this, but I wanted and chose to believe there wasn't. Pike had made the decision to come home, to go out on his own terms, in his own way. He'd chosen his God-given identity, and yes, it spelled the end for him, but at least he'd died happy. At least he wouldn't have to trudge through years and years of pointless life, fighting the urge to get back into drugs, like Olek. Pike would never again have to live in denial of himself.

Part of me wanted to call nine-one-one, but the smarter part of me told me it was a bad idea. What would happen to me if the police came and found my pills, pot, coke, and the remainder of Pike's heroin, not to mention his dead body? It wouldn't be pretty, that was for sure. So, then, the only thing I could think to do was to call Olek.

When he picked up, he said, "Where the hell have you been? I've been calling you all damn day."

"I haven't checked my phone."

"Why'd you hang up on me earlier?"

"Work was busy."

"Whatever, we don't have time for a debate. Listen, Pete checked himself out of Montego this afternoon, and we can't find him anywhere."

It had never occurred to me that Pike could come and go as he pleased. I'd thought rehab was like a prison sentence, that it was some kind of law and you had to stick it out until the end.

"'We?'" I asked. "Who's 'we?'"

"Ambrosia and I. We went to visit him and — "

I laughed sarcastically. "Of course you did. The two of you. Isn't that sweet of you."

Olek, sensing my tone, hesitated. "What are you talking about?"

"I just want you to know that I know. I know everything. And it's all your fault."

"'You *know*?' Know what? What's my fault?"

"You can't just take away everything that means something to someone and expect them to be okay."

"Is this about us helping Pete?"

I laughed again. "'*Helping*' him? Are you serious? Come on, Olek. I know what this is all about. I know why you and Ambrosia put him in rehab."

There was a long and awkward pause then, but I waited him out. Finally Olek said, "I seriously don't know what you're getting at."

I went into the bathroom again and stared at Pike's lifeless body, the now empty pouches next to him where he'd kept his drug. I looked at the charred spoon and the miniature blowtorch. I noticed for the first time a faint burning smell, as of something being cooked too long, a familiar odor since Pike had done his drugs here many times.

"I saw you," I said. "Last night, when you were at Ambrosia's. What was in the bag, a little Chinese, maybe some Italian? Share an intimate dinner?"

Olek laughed then, a genuine laugh as if he was enjoying what I was revealing to him. "Wait. Wait. Do you think we…? Oh my *God*, that's *hilarious*. You've got it all wrong. I met with her to talk about *you*. Remember how you brought it up on the phone a while back? About trying to get clean yourself? We were going over a game plan together, since Pete's so close to being done at Montego. He's been doing great, just *great*. But you're right about one thing. It *was* Chinese. In the bag. We were having dinner and talking about the best way to bring up Montego to you."

I tried to process what he was telling me. I cycled through all the signs: the way Olek's hand moved up and down Ambrosia's arm when Pike overdosed, the way Pike said Ambrosia was acting weird, the seemingly secret meeting last night between Olek and Ambrosia, Olek kissing her at the doorway, Ambrosia closing the curtains. Was I really misinterpreting everything?

"I don't believe you," I said. "You're lying."

"No, I'm not. We care about you. We want you to get better."

"But…but what about Ambrosia acting strange? Pike told me she's been acting funny."

Olek laughed again. "Did Pete also tell you about the conversation they had? The one about her being pregnant and if he didn't get his act together she'd leave him?"

"What?"

"Do you think maybe that's why she's been acting strange around him?"

The air suddenly felt very heavy. It almost took effort to breathe. Pregnant? How could…?

"No," I said. "He…Pike didn't mention that."

"See? Just calm down. It's just a misunderstanding. I'm serious. We want to help you."

I still didn't want to believe it. If Olek was telling the truth, then Pike died because….

I left the bathroom and went to my bedroom, standing with my eyes fixed on the nightstand, where I kept my stash.

"But I'm fine," I said. "I like my life the way

it is. I was just clowning around before, when I said I wanted to get clean."

"Okay, fine. We'll talk more about it later. But back to Pete. Do you know where he is? Any idea at all? It's important we find him, just in case he's having a relapse. I don't think he would, not at this point, but there's always a chance. Have you heard from him at all?"

My nightstand almost seemed to glow in the darkness, as if it had a life force within it and it knew my cravings. I knew that if I opened it, withdrew my stash, the glowing would stop. I also knew that if I went to bed without doing so, the glowing would *never* stop. It would always be there beckoning me, waiting for me to truly accept who I was, because sleep wasn't important, not so important as the high, the high was all there was. The high was all there would ever be. *Come to me*, it called. *Escape in me. Put up the force field. You're safe here. You'll always, always, always be safe here in the spiral.*

"Sorry, Olek," I said. "I have to go."

Before he could respond I hung up, tossed the phone aside, and pulled the nightstand's drawer open. I was sober at the time, hadn't taken anything yet, but I swore it was true: the

Vicodin bottle smiled at me. It had a little face, and it smiled, literally smiled.

I smiled back.

Advent

)———————(

"Stop it, Ron," my sister said. "This has gone on too long."

"Not long enough," I said. "Not when it comes to him."

We were at Mom's, helping her decorate the Christmas tree and to set up her miniature village, all the hand-painted ceramic buildings. Here was a house painted to resemble red brick, a majestic church complete with an impressive steeple, and many more. Mom, always a nerd for arts and crafts, had painted them all.

"All I'm saying," Rhonda went on, "is that it's Christmastime. It won't kill you to give your own father a call."

Mom was in the kitchen putting a collection of cotton balls down on top of the cabinets. The cotton was supposed to be snow, and soon my sister and I would be handing up the village set, piece by piece, and Mom would set them wherever she deemed fit.

"Must you always bicker?" Mom said to us.

"It wouldn't be so bad if Rhonda would get off my ass about Dad." I looked at my sister, who was digging ornaments out of an old cardboard box. "How can you even stand the guy? After all he's *not* done for us?"

"Actually, Ronald, your father has done a lot for you. For *both* of you. He's not the bad guy you make him out to be."

"Mom's right," Rhonda said.

I plopped onto Mom's loveseat and put my hands over my face in a frustrated gesture. "Jesus H. Christ. Are you seriously taking her side, Mom?"

Mom, from up on her stepstool, looked down at me scornfully. "Watch your tone, mister."

Rhonda, who was on her knees rummaging through the ornament box, looked up at me just as scornfully. "Are you going to help me, or…?"

I sighed and leaned forward, joining her on the floor. "I haven't talked to Dad in years.

What's so important about this year compared to last year? You guys weren't giving me shit about it last year."

Rhonda shrugged. "He mentioned your name the other day. He asked about you. I don't really think it's my responsibility to tell him what's going on in your life. I usually do anyways, but I think it's time for you to act like a man and have a conversation yourself. I'm sick of being the middle-girl."

I laughed. "'Act like a man.' Did you really just say that to me?"

Mom said, "Your sister has a point."

I laughed again. "I can't believe this, Mom. After the way Dad fucked you over, you're going to defend him?"

"Didn't I tell you to watch your tone?"

I reached into the box and pulled out a wooden angel that Mom had painted in a cartoonish way, with a myriad of reds and blues and yellows. It had a smiley face and my name painted across its chest, along with the year I was born, 1986.

"I just hate all this 'act like a man' stuff. You're implying that I'm *not* acting like a man, which may or may not be true, I guess, but what

143

about Dad? Is he helpless? He could just as easily pick up the phone and call *me*."

"He has," Mom reminded me.

"Yeah, well. It's been a couple years. If he really cared, he wouldn't give up so easily."

Rhonda placed a blue bulb on the tree and said, "The ball's in your court now. He called you like a thousand times and you never once answered. When was the last time you talked to him, anyways?"

"Who cares?"

I stood up and went to the dining table where Mom had set out a plate full of decorated sugar cookies. I plucked up a Santa Claus and bit his head off.

Mom said, "Your father left me and that was hard on me — on *all* of us — but that was a long, long time ago. We've all moved on, and you and your sister have grown up into decent people. Can't you just let it go and at least *try* to have a positive relationship with him? I just don't want you to regret it someday. I mean, what if he dies tomorrow and you never got a chance to set things straight?"

"Again, Mother, that's not up to me. I'm the neglected son here."

"Dramatic much?" Rhonda said.

Mom laughed and so did I, in spite of myself. "Seriously, though. I just don't think it's up to me to set things right. It's up to him. He's the one that screwed everything up, so he's the one that should fix it. Didn't you always teach us to clean up our own messes, Mom? This is Dad's mess. He should be the one to clean it up."

Mom smiled at me. "Your father and I *both* have cleaned up a lot of *your* messes."

Rhonda laughed. "Me too, me too! Remember when I lent you that fifty-spot when you had that flat tire? Am I ever gonna get that back?"

I stuffed the rest of Santa into my mouth and said, "Bite me."

Mom shook her head in a loving way and said, "My lord, you're more like your father than you even realize."

Dad left Mom for some other woman — Wanda, or Wendy, something like that — when Rhonda and I were nine, almost twenty years earlier. The thing was, Dad had slept with this woman a couple of times and apparently, without consulting with the bitch first, he left

145

Mom and asked her to marry him. Wanda/ Wendy, according to a story Mom told us years later, had laughed in Dad's face. He had misunderstood her intentions and fallen for her when all she wanted was to have an older man as a fuck-buddy.

What was worse was that, after Dad's little transgression blew up in his face, Mom actually waited for him to come back. She was ready to forgive him and move on from it. I was just a little kid, but watching her stare out the front window, waiting for his truck to appear, or helping her set a place for Dad at the dinner table, broke my heart. Not for me, but for her, because she loved him, and when you're a kid you don't know much about love other than that it's supposed to be a magical fairytale.

Dad, newly single and in his mid-thirties, eventually settled into a bachelor's lifestyle, getting drunk and taking home any broad that would pay attention to him. He had a lot of lovers, a lot of different women hanging around when Rhonda and I would visit him while we were growing up. But watching my dad, I came to learn that there was no lover like alcohol, that when everyone else was expendable, alcohol would always be there for you. Just kiss the bottle and slip away into a lustful fantasy. That's why when Mom talked about how Dad never

146

fell in love again, I completely disagreed with her.

I went to the fridge for milk and said, "Got any alcoholic eggnog?" But when I turned around, Rhonda was standing there offering me her cellphone.

"Call him, Ron," she said sadly. "Mom and I are here for you."

I took the phone from her, glared at her with what I hoped was an agitated look on my face, and tossed it into the living room, where it landed atop the sofa with a soft *whump*. "No," I said. "Leave me alone about it."

Rhonda's jaw dropped. "I can't believe you just threw my phone."

Mom said, "Ronald, we're trying to help you. You don't have to be afraid. He's just a person. He'll be glad to hear from you, I know it."

I was getting angrier by the minute. "I just said leave me alone about it."

Seething, I poured a glass of milk, finished it in four long gulps, and then replaced the jug in the fridge. I went back into the living room and started pulling ornaments out of the box, trying to control my frustration. Talking about Dad

147

was enough in itself to set me off, but when it felt like Mom and Rhonda were teaming up on me, I could barely contain my rage.

The house fell silent, and I could feel them staring at me. I wanted nothing more than to lash out at them, to really let them have it, and I was getting dangerously close to doing just that. *One more word*, I thought. *If someone utters one more word about Dad....*

Then Mom said, "He's a good man, Ron. He's made mistakes, but he's — "

I pulled a random glass ornament from the box, stood up, and threw it against the wall. Rhonda and Mom gasped as the bulb shattered, shards spraying in different directions. I glared at Mom and, against the advice of the tiny voice in my head that was almost completely imperceptible at this point, said, "No wonder you're still alone. You deserve it, with that kind of attitude."

Then, without uttering another word, I gathered up my coat and stormed out of the house.

*

Later that evening, as I sat on my laptop adding words to the pointless and awful novel I was working on, my cellphone started buzzing. When I checked it, I saw it was Rhonda and, still fuming, ignored it. I took a long gulp of beer and the phone buzzed again a moment later to indicate Rhonda had left me a voicemail. I began running through the possibilities: "I'm sorry for earlier, Ron." Or maybe, which was more likely, it was, "You're an asshole, Ron." Blah.

The truth was, I was already beginning to feel guilty about my outburst. Of course, Mom and Rhonda knew me well, which meant that they shouldn't have been too surprised to see me lose my temper. But I usually didn't say hateful, disrespectful things. I might punch the wall, or even throw a Christmas ornament, but I'd never say anything cruel to my own mother. I knew what I'd done was wrong, and I knew I'd regret it soon, but I was still angry enough to hang on to the irrational idea that what I'd said was justified.

Then Rhonda called again, and I became even more frustrated and repulsed. I pressed the on-screen ignore button so hard I thought my phone would crack. Seconds later, just after I placed it on my desk, the damn thing started buzzing yet *again*.

This time I answered and said, "Jesus *Christ*,

Rhonda, leave me *alone*."

She didn't answer right away and for a few confusing moments I thought she was breathing into the phone the way someone might do in a horror movie, screwing around with me, maybe trying to get me to laugh, as was always her way when she was ready to make up after a fight. Then it occurred to me that she was actually trying to speak, that she was stumbling over her words, because she was crying.

Any anger I felt instantly melted away. "What? What is it?"

She finally forced a couple words out, her voice breaking in the process. "Mom. It's Mom. She's...her car...." And then everything gave out, and all she could do was sob into my ear.

*

When I arrived at the hospital, my head spinning — I couldn't remember driving there, though the hospital was a half hour from my apartment — Rhonda, Grandma Helen, and Aunt Cheri, Mom's sister, greeted me with an emotional group hug in the ER waiting room. I glanced around and saw five or six other people, their eyes indifferent and tired, as well as an apathetic nurse seated at the front desk. The nurse had her back turned and was joking around with someone else. For some reason, I envied her.

Rhonda wiped tears from her eyes and sniffed. "I'm glad you made it," she said.

"Of course," I said. "How…how bad is it?"

Rhonda burst into tears again and collapsed against Aunt Cheri, who seemed to be holding her composure pretty well. Grandma Helen looked somewhat oblivious — probably in shock.

Aunt Cheri said, "She's in surgery. It's her head. It's…not good."

I shook my head and fought my own emotions. "Jesus. What the hell happened?"

"She just…it looks like she hit a patch of ice out on Higgins Road and rolled her car into one of those deep ditches out there."

"Oh my God. What…where was she going?"

Rhonda pulled her wet face away from Aunt Cheri's shoulder and said, in a remarkably calm yet disbelieving voice, "To the store. She wanted to make more cookies together. I mean, how many times has she been down that road? You know? I…I should've gone with her."

Seeing my twin sister so upset was difficult for me, but I was still trying to process the gravity of what had happened — and I was still angry with her — so it felt like my body wasn't sure which emotion to feel. "Stop it," I said. "That wouldn't have solved anything. If anything you'd be in surgery right now, too."

Grandma Helen, clearly impatient, said, "I wonder if they've heard anything yet," and then waddled up to the front desk, where the apathetic nurse gave her an annoyed look.

I looked at Aunt Cheri and asked, "So it was a single-car accident? No one hit her or anything? She didn't hit anybody?"

Both Aunt Cheri and Rhonda shook their heads. Rhonda said, "One of the houses along Higgins Road, the people that live there saw it happen and called nine-one-one. Then the EMT got a hold of me, and I called you all right away."

I looked at her, unsure about whether or not I should ask the question that was eating at me, but then it slipped out before I could make a conscious decision: "What about Dad? Did you call Dad?"

She nodded and tears welled in her eyes again. "He's on his way. I just can't believe...."

Then she fell against me, and I put my arms around her and rubbed her back gently.

Aunt Cheri, her round face full of pity, touched my hand and said, "I'm going down the hall for some coffee."

The truth was, the severity of what had happened hadn't yet dawned on me. Part of me believed that everyone was being a bit dramatic, that they were exaggerating the extent of Mom's injuries simply because they were worried about her. It wasn't until Grandma Helen came back over and told us that the surgeon was on his way out to talk to us that grief swelled in me. The accident had happened less than two hours before, so they hadn't been in surgery for very long, and that simply couldn't be a good sign. Mom had always picked on me for being too logical, and now I was kicking myself, wishing I could be ignorant to what was about to happen. But even before the surgeon, a kind Indian man who would introduce himself as Dr. Amin, stepped into the waiting room, I knew what to expect, and it was a strange feeling because for those two or three minutes, I was alone in my grief. It was mine, and I had to live in it and protect my family from it.

The surgeon approached us moments after Aunt Cheri returned with her coffee, and the hope I could see in Rhonda's eyes was almost too heartbreaking to endure. I looked around for Dad, but there was no sign of him. Strangely, part of me was glad for it, though I was simultaneously enraged because some irrational part of me believed he should've been there before me, as if he wasn't the most unreliable person I'd ever met.

Rhonda said, "How is she?" and I put my arms around her again.

The surgeon, dressed head to foot in green scrubs, had sad eyes and a gentle demeanor. He introduced himself, explained the procedure he had performed — he'd opened Mom's skull in an effort to relieve pressure and to assuage a cerebral hemorrhage — and then, hesitating, welcomed us all to sit down. I never let go of Rhonda's hand.

"Your mother," he explained, "had a serious brain injury, and we worked on her as hard as possible for as long as possible, but… unfortunately…and I'm so very sorry…her injuries were far too extensive, and we lost her."

Hearing this was, in a weird way, a relief for me, perhaps because I could share in my grief now, because it was no longer mine alone.

There were a few moments of heavy silence

as everyone let Dr. Amin's words sink in. Rhonda's hand tightened around mine, and I could feel her entire body trembling through her touch. I leaned over and grabbed her and, without a word or question of denial, she began to sob uncontrollably into my shoulder.

I mouthed a thank you to Dr. Amin and then whispered again and again to my twin sister, "I'm sorry, I'm sorry, I'm so sorry."

Aunt Cheri and Grandma Helen embraced one another and cried softly, and we all just sat there holding one another for minutes afterwards.

Around an hour later, Dad, the stench of beer on his breath, his face unshaven, his blue eyes bloodshot, finally stumbled in.

"What's going on?" he mumbled, his voice thick with drink. "Where is she?"

I stood up, met his eyes for a moment, and shouldered past him, my collarbone striking his rather painfully, I hoped for both of us.

"Hey," he said. "Where's your mom?"

I stopped at the exit, turned to him, and said, "What the fuck do you care?"

*

Days later, sitting in my rusty old Ford Taurus in a vacant area of St. Paul's Catholic Church parking lot, I was thinking about bowling of all things as I sat behind the wheel, struggling to tighten the Windsor knot in my red tie. It was a relaxed struggle, though. I was wasting time, in no rush to go inside the funeral home. I'd already spent fifteen minutes flipping through radio channels, twisting the knob left and right in my search for a good song, or at least a song that didn't remind me of where I was and what I was doing, watching as groups of other mourners arrived. I hoped Dad wouldn't come — hoped, in fact, that I'd never see him again.

But, at the moment, I was thinking of bowling. And Mom.

As I grew into my twenties, my relationship with Mom developed into a friendship before it began to deteriorate into an acquaintanceship a year or so before she died. Every now and then we still met for drinks at Browner Lanes, the local bowling alley, and threw a few awkward strikes and meandering gutter balls. But it wasn't the same. It was as if she had ceased being my mother. In some way, even, it was as though our roles had begun to reverse, as if in her middle-fifties she had already begun to fall apart, like when an old flower loses its

156

first petal. There was something in the way we conversed, in the way she seemed to subtly beg for my company, that reminded me a day was fast approaching when my mother would become more like my daughter.

But, of course, that day would never come.

What kept me huddled in my car in the parking lot, fighting the urge to twist the top off the fifth of cheap whiskey I'd purchased on the way, was the prospect of seeing my dad inside. Also, because I hadn't attended the showings the previous two days, I was embarrassed about confronting Rhonda and Aunt Cheri. In fact, I'd been intentionally unreachable the previous five days since Mom's accident; I hadn't seen or talked to Rhonda since Mom was pronounced dead at the hospital.

Mom wasn't the only person from whom I'd drifted apart. In fact, in a way, it was as if *I* had come apart, like a Jenga tower. Rhonda, who had been perhaps my closest friend growing up, was more like a stranger now. We were in our late twenties — living our lives, as they say: searching for people to date, working our jobs, and doing a bevy of other things that typical twenty-somethings do. And here we were, twins who were suddenly polar opposites. We should've been sharing in the grief of our mother's tragic death, but some strange instinct in me, some voice inside, warned me to keep my distance — even though we couldn't let go of one another back in the ER. But we'd both needed contact then, we'd needed the support of one another in order to live through that moment. Now we needed our space — or at least *I* did. I knew I wasn't being fair to Rhonda, and that I probably owed it to my mom to be there for my sister, but I was still angry. With both of them. I didn't want to be, but I was.

After some time — probably a half hour or so — the chilly December air finally got to me, so I climbed out of the car. I'd been driving the Taurus since my eighteenth birthday, when my mom had bought it for me (for a little over a thousand bucks). Since then, the old vehicle had deteriorated, but at least it was still running. I kept thinking how ludicrous I probably looked exiting the old rust-bucket, slamming the creaky door. A few folks were smoking just outside the doors of the lovely cobblestone church, taking turns blowing out foggy mixtures of breath and smoke. One of them — a third or fourth or six-hundredth older cousin named Phil, a guy I only knew from various family gatherings throughout the years — watched as I approached. I imagined what he must have thought of me, with my brown hair slicked back, my trimmed beard, my dark suit neatly pressed (I'd opted not to wear my Marmot overcoat), my old rust-stained car. I could feel him judging me. I wondered if he'd attended either of the open-casket showings. If he had, what must he think of me? What did it say about me that I'd not bothered to show my face the past few days?

My nerves rang in my ears like sleigh bells, and I wondered, ridiculously, if it was really the sound of my mom earning her wings. It was probably twenty degrees outside, but I felt warm, flushed with embarrassment and, perhaps, shame. I made eye contact with Phil. He had dark, squinty eyes. He was the type of guy you see that just looks shady, like he was always scrutinizing you.

He nodded at me and smiled wanly, exhaling a long jet of smoke. "Hey, Ron, so sorry for your loss."

Shocked by his genial expression, I nudged past him, in a manner that must have seemed rude, through the church doors, now embarrassed for thinking so lowly of him. "Thanks. Good to see ya," I muttered, in a hurry to free myself from the awkward confrontation.

It was considerably warmer inside St. Paul's. There was the faint sound of organ music, some pretty and arbitrary old church song I'd never know the title to. I wondered if my mom had known it. Mom wasn't particularly religious, but I knew that Rhonda had chosen St. Paul's for the funeral because she was an avid member there. I never knew why my sister had chosen to get involved with a Catholic church, but I suspected an ex-boyfriend had turned her on to the idea.

The church's narthex smelled of pollen and burning candles. There were wreaths and collaged picture boards and myriads of colorful bouquets of flowers placed around the entrance to the sanctuary. I snaked my way through ten or twelve mourners, most of whom were conversing with each other about things unrelated to funerals, and stepped into the sanctuary without glancing at the photographs of my mom on the picture boards.

I took a seat in the last row of pews, next to the center aisle, and looked around. It was probably twenty minutes before the service would begin, so I figured the church was about as full as it would get. I saw Rhonda at the front, conversing with a man and woman I didn't recognize. The casket, just behind my sister, was elevated on the chancel like royal property. It was surrounded by more wreaths and flowers, as well as a few obnoxiously large leafy plants. The priest, a crew-cut, gaunt old man with horn-rimmed glasses, sat in a gaudily decorated chair, over to the right side of the sanctuary, behind the pulpit, where he would deliver the eulogy. A brilliant violet and white chasuble was draped over him. He looked like an elderly king on his throne, looking out over his ignorant minions and subjects.

There were Christmas decorations everywhere. Tiny pine wreaths, each adorned with a prim violet bow, hung off each pew, staring at one another like opposing armies over the main aisle. There was an enormous cross on the far wall, behind the chancel, upon which dangled an emaciated Christ dummy, complete with a crown of thorns and a gory, bright red wound in its side. Above the dummy, someone had hung a beautiful, giant wreath, complete with drooping pinecones and a glittery white bow. The wreath must have been five feet in diameter. It watched over the church like a great eye.

A tall, wide Christmas tree stood beneath the cross and off to the left against the wall, appropriately decorated with alternating violet and white bows, a violet tree skirt with white lining spread out like a dark bloodstain beneath it, and a gaudy, sparkling white star placed atop its peak. It was so festive. I wondered silently what the colors meant and how they related to

Christmas.

Stragglers began to file into the sanctuary, murmuring quietly with one another. I recognized a few of them, including cousin Phil, as the smokers outside. The people who had been standing and conversing in the sanctuary began to take their seats. I did not see Dad anywhere. It wasn't until I exhaled that I realized I'd been holding my breath. Rhonda made her way up the aisle, and I cringed, half hoping she wouldn't notice me. When she saw me, her muddy eyes lit up, as if encountering an old friend. I felt my face flush as she hurried her pace.

My sister looked quite beautiful. In fact, she resembled my mom quite a bit. Her chocolate brown locks were curled, bouncing above her shoulders with each step she took. And while she wasn't as thin as Mom — Rhonda fretted outwardly about her weight rather often — she looked confident, strong, which reminded me of Mom. While I'd been passively aware of the hollow feeling of loss in my stomach for the past few minutes, I didn't truly feel sad until the moment my sister approached me.

"Ronald!" she said playfully, almost yelling. "Where have you been? I've been worried sick!" It was as if she'd completely forgotten

162

about our fight.

I stood up and accepted her embrace, which was brief and awkward. She was damp, sweaty. Her hair smelled like an apple orchard, sweet like cider, yet beneath that, sour like rotting fruit. "Around," I said, meaning just the opposite. "Working on my book."

"Well, Aunt Cheri was looking for you. Oh, and we *really* need to talk."

"Talk?"

"About funeral costs and stuff. Okay?"

I shrugged. "Whatever."

She put her hands on my shoulders in a compassionate way. "Listen, I'm *so* busy, but the funeral's about to start. You should go up front and sit there. Aunt Cheri's saving you a seat."

"Nice of her," I said, trying not to look at Mom's casket. I felt lucky that Mom's head wasn't raised. I didn't want to see her face. Not that I would've been able to see it very well from where Rhonda and I stood.

"I'm going outside to get everyone in here," Rhonda said, sliding past me towards the narthex. "I'll be up there in a minute!"

163

"Okay, sure," I said, watching as she rushed out. Her dress, the purple hue of a fading sunset, fluttered behind her, as if an angelic breeze had suddenly burst through the entryway.

Instead of joining Aunt Cheri up front, I sat down in the same pew and faced forward. The mahogany casket shimmered under the soft lemon lighting, mocking me. I knew I should move to the front to sit by my family, but I felt more comfortable alone. I saw the backs of Aunt Cheri's dark brown head, as well as the blue-gray bouncy curls of Grandma Helen's perm. I'd felt badly for her ever since Grandpa Jack passed away nine years earlier. But Grandma Helen was still as lively and sweet as ever — well into her seventies, but so full of life, despite losing her husband of forty-something years. I noticed the slight bob of her shoulders and realized she must be crying. I couldn't take it, so I looked away, back to the priest sitting on his throne. He looked so…bored. My mom deserved better than this. She deserved to have someone who loved her deliver the eulogy. It was an intimate thing to summarize someone's life and priests were, as I understood them, so indifferent. This was their job: "Rest in peace. Thank you, drive through."

*

The funeral service was long and boring, but I left with the feeling that it had been too short, that not enough had been said about my mom. Rhonda had returned rushing down the center aisle, but she'd only waved and smiled sadly at me as she passed by. To my surprise, somewhere between prayers, the priest — Father Angelo, as I came to learn later — stepped aside to let Rhonda say a few words about Mom. I tried to ignore most of what she was saying, as if not hearing her words would mean I'd never have to let go of Mom, but one part of her speech stuck with me.

My sister, always a crier, did quite well avoiding crying. I glanced up from time to time, trying my best not to hear what memories she was sharing, or what special characteristic about Mom she was highlighting. But there, at the end of her eulogy, I caught something. Rhonda, clearly fighting back tears, her face puckering exactly the way Mom's used to when she cried, said, "…that Mom would tell us all to live happy and laugh much."

In that moment, it occurred to me that I hadn't "lived happy" in quite some time — if ever. I felt insubstantial, as if I hadn't lived at all, let alone unhappily. I wanted to leave then — not just St. Paul's, but the entire disapprobation of my life in small-town

Michigan — to vanish without uttering one word of goodbye to anyone. This realization, of my ability to disappear, was both terrifying and alluring, and I wondered if my dad had felt the same inexorable emotion when he'd left us all those years ago. He must have. For the first time that I could remember, I pitied him a little — and perhaps missed him.

After the funeral, I left quickly, before anyone could stop me and utter some half-hearted or false expression of condolence, and drove into the dull, nearly undetectable December sunset towards Mom's house. I wasn't sure why I was going there; my head told me it was more reasonable to get back to my apartment and pack up. But I had to see the place, the unfinished Christmas decorations inside — I had to feel the death of it.

It was about a twenty-minute drive, so by the time I arrived, it had already grown dark. I parked at the end of the driveway, as I always had, out near the lonely country road. I cut the engine and twisted open the bottle of cheap whiskey I'd left sitting on the worn gray passenger's seat. The car filled with a hollow, metallic ticking sound as the engine began to wind itself down, and I was overcome by the feeling of a journey ending — a journey ending so that another might begin. I swigged the whiskey, stifling a cough as the spicy fluid trickled its way down my throat into my cold belly.

Strangely, I felt no regret for going against custom and refusing to approach my mom's corpse at the end of the service, all stiff and already decaying in its snooty mahogany eternal deathbed. I wondered haphazardly how much the damn casket cost — how much the entire *funeral* cost — and hoped Rhonda wouldn't ask me for any money as she'd suggested before the service began. As quickly as the thought came, however, I dismissed it, because I'd already made up my mind that I was leaving this place, tomorrow, forever. I'd sell whatever I didn't need and move on to some distant western horizon where the air was always warm and the heart was never empty. I'd hole up in some apartment in Arizona where I could read and write and be alone all I wanted, without being judged as if it were some great crime to choose not to love.

I took a thicker pull of whiskey and climbed out of the rusty Taurus, making my way up the driveway towards the garage. Mom's house — the very house I'd grown up in, the very house I'd stormed out of just days earlier — was a comfortable bi-level with brown vinyl siding and a steep, black-shingled roof. A great bay window and two smaller windows watched the street from the second floor. There were also two more small windows beneath the bay window, to the left of the porch and front door. Over to the right of the porch was the garage. Each window had faux shutters on either side of it, painted white to match the front door. As I approached, a memory floated up into my consciousness: my mom and I, fifteen years ago or so, tossing the baseball around in the front yard. I remembered the crack of my mitt and the dull snap of my mother's as we took turns throwing and catching the ball. I was glad to have those nostalgic sounds echoing in my memory…but I was also angry, resentful. It felt like another activity I'd missed out on, an activity that was supposed to be between fathers and sons. Yes, I had stayed at Dad's house quite a few times while growing up — as many times as required by law — but we'd never once that I could remember tossed the baseball around.

I came to the porch steps and located my mom's house key on my keychain, but then stopped in my tracks. I hadn't noticed, but my dad was sitting there, in the dark, at the top of the steps, leaning back against the front door. He had on a red hooded sweatshirt and dark blue jeans. For the first time in many, many years I noticed just how much we resembled each other.

It was as if an older me, from the future, had come back in time to confront himself. Dad had even grown a beard since I'd seen him the night Mom died, although his wasn't as full or well-groomed as mine.

He didn't say anything at first; he just sat there, staring at the sky.

"How'd you get here?" I asked, looking for a vehicle.

"Cab," he said. I hesitated, unsure of how to confront the man who had broken me, now that I was alone with him. Then he said, "There's no stars. It's just...black. Empty."

A light snow began to fall. "Why'd you take a cab?" I asked.

He looked at me and smiled. Although it was dark, I could see that his eyes were puffy, as if he'd been crying. "Lost my license a few months ago. It's why I was late getting to the hospital last week, too." He laughed, a more genuine sound than the moment demanded, as if something about the situation was hilarious. "It's a bitch, son. I'm telling you, it's a real fucking bitch."

"Don't call me son," I said, trying my best to sound disgusted and not intimidated by his presence. "You lost that right a long, long time ago."

My dad raised his hands to the sky and said in a silly voice, quoting *Star Wars*, "A long, long time ago, in a galaxy *farrrr awayyyy*...." He gave a sigh that resembled a laugh.

"Dad," I said, trying to figure out if I should move forward or step back. "Dad, what's going on?"

"You know why Catholic churches use purple around Christmastime?"

I shook my head.

"It's the color they use during advent. Those assholes have all these...." He waved his hands around sarcastically. "These fucking *traditions*."

Something Mom had said came to me then, a little quip she'd thrown in during our argument the day she died: *My lord, you're more like your father than you even realize*. And I was. I really, really was. I could see it in his mannerisms, hear it in his voice and in the reproachful way he talked about other people.

"Wait," I said, coming to a realization. "Were you there today? At the funeral?"

He nodded. "Yeah. I was. I stood back in

170

the *narthex*." He made quotation marks with his fingers.

"I didn't see you."

"Didn't want you to. I didn't even want your sister to see me."

He leaned forward then, unexpectedly, cradled his face in his hands, and began to sob rather loudly. I looked around, embarrassed for him, but then moved closer to him. I sat beside him and placed a reluctant arm around his shoulder.

He squirmed out of my grasp and drew back. "I've been losing things — *people* — my whole life," he said, his voice cracking.

"I know how you feel," I told him, and looked away, blinking away my own tears.

"Do you," he said more than asked, as if he didn't believe me. "The thing is, Ronald, I never realized it was my own goddamn fault until…." He took a deep breath and choked on his words. "Until *now*." He shook his head and looked off into the distance, a disgusted look pulling at the corners of his face. "It's too late," he said glumly, and buried his face in his hands again.

As I watched him, my heart swelled with a foreign emotion, something both warm and sorrowful. I pulled my dad close, marveling at his frailty, and looked out across the road, into the open field where old Farmer Jackson would plant his corn again next year. I ran my hand through Dad's hair as though he'd done something to warrant my love, as if every part of me, down to my core, didn't want to hate him.

"Don't leave me, son," he said, his voice falling to a strained whisper, with an intensity that sent a chill down my spine. "We can just… figure something out. Right? Can't we just…I don't know…*go back*?"

He wrapped his arms around me and pulled me against him tightly. His touch sapped my anger, and I began to cry softly. The wind picked up, whistling through the barren trees on either side of the house. We held each other there hopefully, cautious, the wind and the snow and the empty house pulling us in different directions, waiting for one of us to apologize.

WordpoolPress.com

Other titles from Wordpool Press:

Seventh of Eleven
by Dorothy Sabean

Creative Wordsmithing
by Bill De Herder

Dinner with Doppelgangers
by Colleen Wells

 Find Wordpool Press on Facebook!